Thunder rumbled and a flash of lightning briefly lit the gloom as she walked toward the stairwell of her apartment.

A footfall registered, out of sync with hers. She paused to listen, but almost instantly shook off the paranoia that gripped her. What she'd heard was probably an echo.

Another footfall sounded, this time sharply distinct. A raw flash of alarm went through her. A hand snaked out of the darkness and closed on her arm, wrenching her to a halt. Her arm jerked in automatic reflex as she spun, teeth bared, and stepped into her attacker, throwing him off balance as she snapped her elbow into a face eerily blacked out by a balaclava. He grunted with pain and released his hold.

In that instant she flung herself toward the elevator. A hand snagged at her jacket. Gritting her teeth, she jerked free. Relief flooded her as light flared across the bare expanse of concrete, spotlighting her in its beam. Gabriel West's startled gaze locked with hers [illegible] ht exploded in her [illegible]

Dear Reader,

Our exciting month of May begins with another of bestselling author and reader favorite Fiona Brand's Australian Alpha heroes. In *Gabriel West: Still the One*, we learn that former agent Gabriel West and his ex-wife have spent their years apart wishing they were back together again. And their wish is about to come true, but only because Tyler needs protection from whoever is trying to kill her—and Gabriel is just the man for the job.

Marie Ferrarella's crossline continuity, THE MOM SQUAD, continues, and this month it's Intimate Moments' turn. In *The Baby Mission*, a pregnant special agent and her partner develop an interest in each other that extends beyond police matters. Kylie Brant goes on with THE TREMAINE TRADITION with *Entrapment*, in which wickedly handsome Sam Tremaine needs the heroine to use the less-than-savory parts of her past to help him capture an international criminal. Marilyn Tracy offers another story set on her Rancho Milagro, or Ranch of Miracles, with *At Close Range*, featuring a man scarred—inside and out—and the lovely rancher who can help heal him. And in Vickie Taylor's *The Last Honorable Man*, a mother-to-be seeks protection from the man she'd been taught to view as the enemy—and finds a brand-new life for herself and her child in the process. In addition, Brenda Harlan makes her debut with *McIver's Mission*, in which a beautiful attorney who's spent her life protecting families now finds that *she* is in danger—and the handsome man who's designated himself as her guardian poses the greatest threat of all.

Enjoy! And be sure to come back next month for more of the best romantic reading around, right here in Intimate Moments.

Leslie J. Wainger
Executive Senior Editor

Gabriel West: Still the One

FIONA BRAND

INTIMATE MOMENTS™
Published by Silhouette Books
America's Publisher of Contemporary Romance

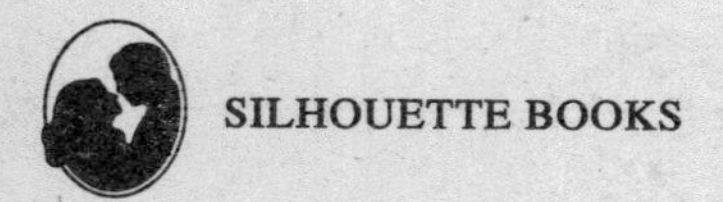

ISBN 0-373-27289-8

GABRIEL WEST: STILL THE ONE

This edition published by arrangement with Harlequin Books S.A.

Visit Silhouette at www.eHarlequin.com

Printed in U.S.A.

Books by Fiona Brand

Silhouette Intimate Moments

Cullen's Bride #914
Heart of Midnight #977
Blade's Lady #1023
Marrying McCabe #1099
Gabriel West: Still the One #1219

Silhouette Books

Sheiks of Summer
"Kismet"

FIONA BRAND

has always wanted to write. After working eight years for the New Zealand Forest Service as a clerk, she decided she could spend at least that much time tying to get a romance novel published. Luckily, it only took five years, not eight. Fiona lives in a subtropical fishing and diving paradise called the Bay of Islands with her two children.

For Crazy Horse—
for the magic of who he is, his courage and spirit,
his uncanny immunity during battle. He's my inspiration
for Gabriel West and one of my all-time heroes.

Chapter 1

Port Moresby, Papua New Guinea

The man walked out of the night, moving without haste, yet not dawdling, his gait fluid, smooth. He was big and sleek with muscle, his broad shoulders stretching his black T-shirt tight so that it clung like a second skin. The subtle arrogance to the tilt of his head, the gleam of light sliding over the taut swell of biceps, warned anyone who gave him so much as a passing glance that he wasn't an easy mark. He carried no discernable firearm, but then he didn't need an overt display of firepower; the body itself was a weapon.

The yellowish glare of a streetlamp slid over deceptively sleepy amber eyes and exotic cheekbones, a full, beautiful mouth framed by a square, stubbled jaw. A dark, masculine mane hung loose about his shoulders, accentuating the impression of danger.

The man was beautiful in the mesmerizing way of a fallen angel; the looks were a rare gift and a curse that had taught him early on to defend himself, then later, to assert enough dominance to ensure that he was left alone. The fact that his name was Gabriel was pure chance, a whim on the part of a mother who wasn't sure which one of her paying customers had fathered him, or what had possessed her to carry the child to full term in the first place. Whichever way you looked at it, Gabriel West considered himself to have little in common with angels, fallen or otherwise.

Ahead, light slicked along metal as a car door swung open. West's head came up, nostrils flaring, drinking in the steamy tropical scents of city and night as he deliberately let his mind drift, picking up on peripherals. A flicker of movement across the street signaled the presence of one of Renwick's mercenaries. The inky darkness off to the left was a dead-end alley. Renwick would have placed another man there.

His lips barely moved as he relayed the information to the mobile unit that had shadowed him as far as the street corner, the dull black van blending with the night and the shabby conglomeration of buildings that lined the docks and signaled the edge of what passed for the red-light district in this town. The tiny state-of-the-art communication device masquerading as a stud in his ear gave two bursts of static in response, indicating that McKee, Sawyer and Lambert were in place.

He strolled from light into shadow, then back into light again, his gait unaltered as he passed the point of no return. He was committed.

Ahead, Renwick uncurled himself from the low-slung curves of a late-model Maserati. The door swung closed with an expensive thunk. The arms dealer was lean, dapper, ostensibly relaxed—on target for another profitable night. Everything was going to plan. Something was wrong.

Adrenaline pumped: West's gut clenched in reflex. Renwick was alone; the absence of visible support was wrong. Somehow, in the few hours that had passed since their preliminary meeting in Renwick's drab downtown office, the deal had gone sour.

He relayed the warning, knowing as he did so that the team would move in, poised to get him out if they could. Not that a clean rescue was probable now; he was well within Renwick's circle of influence.

His options weren't good. He could go for cover, and risk being pinned down, maybe even shot before the other team members could get to him, or he could keep his cool, get in close, use the car as a shield and Renwick for collateral to negotiate his ass out of there.

The cold warning increased the closer he got to

Renwick, culminating in a preternatural tingle that stirred along the length of his spine and settled at his nape. He could feel the impending combat, almost taste it.

West felt the familiar shift inside, the peculiar calmness that came with battle—an altered state that freed him to act and react without conscious thought—and the odd, light-headed sensation, as if a part of him had drifted free, a cold observer to the act. He didn't question the shift; it was as natural to him as breathing, a survival mechanism that had been in place since childhood, and one he'd consciously honed with years of meditation and martial arts. Odd as it seemed, the cold discipline required for both activities had dovetailed perfectly with the despair and savagery of his upbringing, binding the drifting, disparate parts of his being into a formidable whole. He'd learned early on to fight with everything that he had, and that included his mind. No matter how much edge he gave himself with weapons and a well-trained body, there was always someone bigger waiting to take him down.

A trickle of sweat eased down his spine. The muted thud of his boots hitting the pavement echoed dully, the sound almost instantly absorbed into the heavy press of the night.

He carried a knife in a spine sheath, another in a custom-made slot in his boot. A pocket-sized Walther was strapped to his left ankle; the small-calibre sidearm as slick a piece of hell as he'd ever handled. The meet with Renwick stipulated no firearms. Naturally, West had ignored the stipulation. Strolling into an arms deal without the benefit of a semi-automatic was about as close to naked as he ever wanted to get.

Renwick's head lifted in a brief signal of recognition, his gaunt face taking on a yellowish hue in the glare of the sodium streetlamp, his dark gaze hooded. West noted the bulge under his left arm. He was carrying—naturally—a handgun so big it was wrecking the line of his jacket.

Grim humor dissolved the tension knotting his belly. Oh yeah, Renwick was an asshole: no style, no class.

A surge of recklessness flowered inside West, shafted through him on a hot, savage beat. His mouth curved in a slow, cold smile and he resisted the urge to close his eyes and ride out the hot feeling. That would get him killed for sure.

God, he was crazy. Certifiable. Renwick was itching to use some of the second-hand Russian weaponry he'd been hawking all through Indonesia and the South Pacific, and in the next few minutes he probably would. West could die, and he was suddenly enjoying himself, so alive he could hardly bear it, the rush better than sex. If the SAS psych team ever got their hands on him they'd lock him up and throw away the key.

A door popped open midway along the stretch of pavement between West and Renwick. Light flared across the street as two women emerged from a warehouse that, at four-thirty in the morning, should have been deserted. The door swung closed, the flat sound broken by the click of high heels on concrete.

The unexpectedness of the intrusion threw West off balance; his attention was caught by the tawny swing of hair shimmering around the first woman's shoulders, the pure line of her profile.

Tyler.

The shock of recognition hit him like a belly punch even as his mind rejected the information. Tyler couldn't be here. She was safe in New Zealand, thousands of miles away, but the notion persisted as the woman lifted a startled hand to sweep hair from her face.

A shadowy blur of movement snapped West's gaze back to Renwick. He caught the dull gleam of a gun in the arms dealer's hand.

He cursed, going wild inside, even as his fingers closed on the throwing knife. The woman whirled, face swamped by shadows. The glitter of her eyes clashed with West's as Renwick's arm came up.

Slow. He was too damned slow.

The thought hung in West's mind as the knife flashed through the air and he dove, taking the woman down onto the pavement with him. In that split second he registered the flat report of the gun, once, twice—Renwick crumpling.

His shoulder slammed into the pavement, but he barely noticed the shock of the fall as he rolled free of the limp weight of the woman and came up into a crouch, the Walther in his hand. He fired across the street, then into the mouth of the alley, berating himself for not following his instincts and carrying a nine-millimetre weapon. The Walther was cool, but it was strictly a close-quarters weapon—short-barreled and light, the magazine fully loaded with only six shells.

Brick exploded behind him, showering him with fragments. A high-pitched moan, more animal than human, pierced the thick heaviness of the night as the second woman scrambled for the door she'd walked out of just seconds ago. West's stomach knotted as he snaked, belly-flat, to reach the still form of the woman, the keening moan spinning him back to his years on the streets when he'd been little more than a child, fighting to eat, sometimes fighting to breathe after he'd endured beatings that had come close to killing him.

The cloying scents of blood and fear and cheap perfume flooded his nostrils as he clamped her slight body against his and crawled to the cover of Renwick's car. She was still alive; he could hear the sound of her breathing, faint and very rapid, laced with a liquid rattle. His stomach knotted as he eased her flat beneath the wash of the streetlamp. Renwick had fired twice. One of those bullets had hit the woman. The large-calibre round had pierced her ribcage, shattering bone and tearing an exit wound beneath one arm.

Cursing beneath his breath, he laid his gun down and propped her upright against the car, elevating the wound in an attempt to stem the flow of blood. Her head lolled as he tore his T-shirt off and bunched it over her chest and beneath her arm, applying what pressure he could without adding to her injuries, but the tell-tale sponginess indicated massive soft-tissue damage, and that more than one rib had been broken. With every shuddering rise and fall of her chest, fluid aspirated into her lungs. She was literally drowning in her own blood.

The roar of a vehicle accelerating down the street snapped West's head up. The van fishtailed and shunted the back of Renwick's car, riding up on the pavement and almost hitting West in the process. Disbelief punched through West. Carter, the crazy bastard, had come to get him out.

The street erupted with gunfire. The crack of a rifle shot bounced off the stained facades of warehouses and dilapidated shop frontages. The sharp rat-tat-tat of rounds hitting metal punctuated the tortured whine of a ricochet. The stench of cordite hung in the air, an acrid contrast to the salt tang of the sea and the pervasive smell of rancid fish oil from the nearby docks.

The van door was flung wide. Carter swore, his voice gravelly as he flowed out onto the pavement and kicked the door shut with one booted foot. The moment took on a surreal quality as West pressed his fingers to the side of the woman's throat, searched for a pulse, and didn't find one.

A woman had just died, and Carter was bitching about who was going to pay for the van.

More gunshots sounded, followed by a flurry of automatic fire. Minutes later the street was silent, the absence of sound faintly shocking.

It was over.

West didn't question the sense of finality that settled inside him, or the spookiness that went with knowing. To him, his gut reactions were simply an extension of the physical reflexes he'd trained into his body, and over the years he'd learned to trust in them.

Gently, he let the woman go, sat back on his heels and let out a breath.

He studied her face in the wash of the streetlight, abruptly curious. He touched her cheek. She wasn't the wife he'd walked out on five years ago, but she was someone, and she'd taken a bullet that had been meant for him. He was covered in her blood.

Gently, he laid her flat on the sidewalk, retrieved his damp, stained T-shirt and reached for dispassion.

Carter's hand landed on his shoulder. He heard his voice, recognized the soothing rumble. This was a job, and the lady—a hooker—had been in the wrong place at the wrong time.

It had been quick, one second she'd been there, panicked gaze locked on his, the next...

The crazy thing was, she hadn't even looked like

Tyler. She'd walked like her, had that long pretty hair, a certain way of holding her head. That was all it had taken and he'd lost it. Dropped the ball.

Sweet Jesus... West lurched to his feet, turned aside from the two bodies, Renwick's still oddly elegant in death. He ran the fingers of one hand through his hair, took a deep breath, and then another, and something broke apart inside him, an essential hardness as much a part of him as flesh and bone. For years he'd walked an edge, caught between not caring, and caring too much...a hungry street kid's recipe for survival. And like the street-smart kid he'd once been, he still reached for the cool not to feel. Feelings shoved you off balance, opened you up....

He knew what was happening—it had been creeping up on him for months. There was even a name for it: battle fatigue. He was tired, his commitment for the job gone. He was still sharp, but it was becoming more and more of an effort to maintain the level of focus and acuity required for active undercover operations. Whatever he chose to label it, the fact remained—he'd been in the military too long.

Two members of the team, McKee and Sawyer, melted out of the darkness, followed seconds later by the fifth and final member, Lambert. Lambert made brief, neutral eye contact with West. McKee and Sawyer both gave him a wide berth.

West didn't bother with the mental shrug. He had a reputation for being cold and distant—a little scary.

He never did anything to alter that impression because the solitude suited him. He'd never been anything but a loner, and at thirty-one years of age the pattern was ingrained. He had friends, some of them as close as he was ever likely to get to actually having family, but essentially he was alone.

He examined the tinge of gray lightening the grim canyon of the street, turned toward what passed for sunrise in this city of heat and humidity and jungle mists. In half an hour this place would be a steam bath, the sun dominating a hot, clear sky, the streets teeming with raucous life.

He'd come close to not seeing it.

Lambert handed him his knife. West took the blade, cleaned it on his T-shirt, then methodically slipped it back into its spine sheath. Carter tossed him a bottle of water, took his cell phone out and called in an ambulance. West tipped his head back and drank, wiped his mouth with the back of his hand, then tipped water over his naked torso to clean off the blood. He became aware that Lambert was surreptitiously watching him—read the repelled fascination in the man's eyes. Lambert was a rookie, ten years younger and fresh-faced—a nice boy doing a dirty job. He hadn't liked handling the knife, or the way Renwick and the woman had died.

There was blood everywhere, still smeared across West's chest, streaking the backs of his hands. His hair was tangled around his face, sticking to his shoulders. He must look like a damn vampire…not someone Lambert, or the other two, would ever want to get comfortable with.

A hot blast of emotion threatened to burn through his icy calm. Not someone that the majority of the human race would ever be comfortable with, come to that.

Something of what he was feeling must have registered with the younger man. His gaze slid away, locked on the body of the woman lying on the ground. Abruptly, he wheeled and joined Sawyer and McKee in the back of the van.

West knew what was going through Lambert's mind. Over the years he'd garnered a reputation for being lucky—of having some kind of magical immunity, so that when everything went to hell West walked away with barely a scratch. There were men who wouldn't work with him because that fact spooked them. They figured they'd be the ones to die.

Not for the first time West worried at his own apparent good luck. The fact was he had a reckless streak—a bad, bad habit that kept him choosing risky assignments and walking the edge. In a numbers game, he'd long since played out the odds. Sometimes the way he was scared him. He'd gotten too cold, too fatalistic about dying.

He eyed the steadily increasing glow in the east, felt the first touch of heat burning through the early-morning mists.

He hadn't felt cold or fatalistic when he'd thought

it was Tyler on the street. Fear had lashed through him. Every cell in his body had reacted.

His jaw clenched against a replay of the panic that had shafted through him when he'd thought his wife was about to walk straight into the barrel of Renwick's gun. In that moment a part of him had gone wild. He hadn't cared if Renwick's bullets had slammed into his chest; all he'd wanted to do was save Tyler.

He took another deep breath, easing the tension in his belly. Suddenly, he felt old and tired, sick of death and meanness. He wanted...home.

Oh, yeah, he thought grimly, that would undo him. He had no business even thinking about home, or about Tyler.

As he swung into the van and snapped the door closed, he wondered what Tyler was doing now—this very second. He hadn't so much as glimpsed her for months.

An abrupt hunger to be with the woman he'd walked out on, but never succeeded in forgetting, ate at him, sharp and deep. Temper erupted and he swore beneath his breath.

Carter glared at him as he started the van and reversed, disengaging from the totaled rear of Renwick's car with a squeal of torn metal. "What's wrong with you?"

"Nothing."

Carter changed gear and accelerated onto the street, barely missing clipping the mangled Maserati.

"You're crazy, that's what's wrong. I shouldn't have let you walk down that street. You've got a damned death wish."

"If anyone's got a death wish, it's the guy *driving* this clapped-out van." West strapped on his seat belt. When Carter was behind the wheel, he was the safest guy on the planet.

"My *driving* saved your sorry ass."

West couldn't argue with that. Carter had driven the van into the center of the firefight, risking his own safety to provide West with cover. The van had taken the brunt of the fire and now resembled nothing so much as a colander. The rental firm would have a hernia, and Carter had bought himself a good day's worth of paperwork and grief trying to justify the expenditure.

Carter braked at an intersection. Cars had begun to fill the streets—early morning commuters and taxis heading for the airport to catch passengers off the red-eye flights. A truck loaded with melons shifted down a gear and eased through the intersection, heading for the markets. Port Moresby was waking up.

An aging ambulance screamed past them, lights flashing. A cold chill chased across West's skin, twitched deep in his belly, even though the ambient temperature was warm. He lifted a hand to his face, rubbed compulsively at his temples.

A fine tremor ran through his hands. He let out a breath. That was shaky, too.

He was going into shock.

Oh, jeez...damn. Tyler.

A hot pain burst to life in the center of his chest. That's what had done it. He'd thought it was her, and now he was going to pieces.

He closed his eyes and let his head drop back onto the cracked vinyl of the seat. The breath sifted from between his teeth. Tyler.

He *was* going crazy. The psych team would chew him up, spit him out, and that was if he didn't get himself committed first.

Lately—the last couple of months—as hard as he'd tried, he couldn't stop thinking about her.

Chapter 2

One month later, Auckland, New Zealand.

Gabriel West was back in her life.

Dr. Tyler Laine's fingers slipped on her laptop keyboard. The machine beeped, and a cartoon character popped onto the screen. A little balloon message sprang out of the side of its head, politely asking if she needed help.

For long seconds, Tyler stared blankly at the ridiculous creature with its cheerful face, her overtired mind abruptly incapable of grasping the simple actions required to close the help file.

She'd been making lists, staring at lists, for hours, trying to shed some light on the mystery of who had walked into her family's vault and stolen a set of ancient jade artifacts that had been under her care for the past three months, before her reputation and her career were shredded beyond redemption. She needed to make sense of a burglary that didn't make any kind of normal sense.

The jade pieces were unique, *priceless,* but it wasn't so much the quality of the objects, but their age and the mystery shrouding them that had caught and held the attention of experts and collectors alike.

Jade, like many minerals, could generally be traced to its country of origin. It was simply a matter of profiling the mineral content and then matching it up with the characteristics exhibited by jade from different countries or locations. Sometimes the jade could even be traced to the particular mine it had come from. The set of three objects had been analyzed and identified as extraordinarily high-quality nephrite, originating from the Sinkiang region in China. The objects: belt and scabbard accoutrements, and a round vessel carved in the shape of a bird, had also been dated. They were neolithic in origin and had been carved approximately three and a half thousand years ago, during the Shang dynasty. All three pieces were old enough, and rare enough, to be the jewel in any collection without the added mystery of how they had come to be included with Maori grave goods on the small island nation of Aotearoa, New Zealand, thousands of miles away from China.

It wasn't unusual for artifacts to be stolen from museums, or looted from archeological sites. The theft of artifacts from war-torn countries was rife. But it was unusual for anyone to want to steal artifacts that were so world-renowned they could never hope to display them.

Anger flickered, warming her, but even that emotion had become faded, distant, as exhaustion closed in on her, sucking the last remnants of her vitality so that she simply sat, motionless, her eyes fixed on the screen until the minute irritation of the electronic flicker made her blink.

A fine tremor ran through her, jerking her back to an awareness of just how punchy she'd become. Her mind was functioning, barely, but her body was closing down; her pulse slow, viscid—her breathing shallow and long-drawn-out.

She hadn't slept more than four hours in the last seventy-two, and she couldn't remember when she'd last eaten anything that could remotely pass for a square meal. She could remember taking a few bites of a sandwich in the half-hour respite she'd had between police interviews that afternoon, but she couldn't for the life of her recall what had been in the sandwich. She'd been having trouble concentrating all day, her mind blanking out for short periods of time. If she closed her eyes now, she would fall asleep in her chair.

Her hand found the mouse, her fingers stiff and clumsy as she moved it on the pad until she located the electronic cursor on the screen, then centered it on the cartoon character.

Help.

She took a deep breath, then let it out slowly. ''If you've got an FBI unit on hold...maybe.''

She clicked the mouse, bringing up the menu, then closed the file, sending the little intruder back into its hidey-hole.

Right now she could use the FBI, Interpol, the CIA, a SWAT team...whatever.

Letting out a breath, she hooked off her spectacles, sat back from the bright glow of light pooling her desk and ran a hand over her sleek knot of hair to loosen the tension.

The list of private collectors she'd been compiling from Laine's sales records dating back for the past ten years was starkly illuminated by the bluish glow of the screen. The names could have been written in Chinese characters for all the good it did her.

Her eyelids drooped again, and a picture of West strolling toward his car as she'd left for work this morning floated into her mind and she blinked, banishing the image.

She desperately needed to work, to focus, but the fact that the husband who had walked out on her five years ago was now practically her next-door neighbor kept distracting her, so that she found herself staring into space, precious minutes out of her long working day lost.

Her stomach rumbled. Frowning, she checked her watch. Almost eight. Past time she was out of here.

''Cancel the FBI unit.'' She smothered a yawn as

she saved the file to a disk. ''What I need is an analyst.''

The tawny gleam of light off an egg-shaped tiger's-eye worry stone caught her eye as she waited for her computer to shut down. Absently, Tyler picked it up, her fingers smoothing the silky curves, her mind abruptly shifting back to a time, eight years ago, when she'd been mesmerized by eyes that had burned with the same intense shades of gold.

Gabriel.

Dispassionately, she examined the tension that held her motionless when all she wanted to do was leave the office, drive home, ransack the fridge for a snack, then crawl into bed and forget that the world she'd so carefully constructed around herself since she was eight years old was coming apart.

She was crazy even to examine the past. Five years ago she'd asked West to leave, and the husband she'd never been able to tame had packed his bags and walked, leaving for another secret assignment in some foreign country—preferring the edgy danger of the SAS, the hardship and the uncertainties—maybe even a bullet in the dark—to spending time with her.

For months she'd clung to the fantasy that he'd come back.

Well, he had come back. She just hadn't ever imagined it would be five years later, and that they'd be *neighbors.*

Jerkily, Tyler set the tiger's-eye stone down. The gleam of the worry stone continued to draw her eye as she slipped the disk into a side pocket in her handbag, unplugged her laptop and placed it into her briefcase along with the notes she'd made. She snapped the case closed and picked it up by the grip, hooked her handbag over her shoulder and rose to her feet.

She should have gotten rid of the tiger's eye years ago. She must have thrown it away a dozen times, only to pull it out of the bin and dust it off. The problem was that it was irritatingly beautiful. The hot flashes of gold and copper always caught at her and she just couldn't bring herself to chuck something so elegant and enduring away.

Her problem was she never could let go, never could throw away something she'd cherished, even if the cherishing was well in the past. Once she loved someone or something, she hung on for grim death. When it came to relationships, her loyalty wasn't in question, just her sanity.

Which was probably why she'd never quite been able to cut West out of her life.

The thought hit her square in the chest, literally stopping her in her tracks. The possibility—however remote—that West could still have some call on her emotions.

Uh-oh. No way. She didn't still care for West.

There were lots of reasons why she shouldn't even *like* him...if she ever thought of him at all, although the last few months, crazy as it seemed, she hadn't been able to stop thinking about him. It was as if her mind had been caught up in some kind of loop. She'd even dreamed about him, which was beyond strange, because she hadn't glimpsed him more than a handful of times in as many years.

She'd attributed the phenomena to stress and a ticking biological clock. She was twenty-eight, alone, and still tied to a marriage with West for the simple reason that neither of them had bothered to dissolve it.

Maybe it was cowardly, but she'd become used to living in relationship limbo, and had even welcomed it at times because it was a convenient shield when all she'd wanted to do after West had left was crawl into a dark hole and hide. It had taken her months to feel even remotely normal, and then she'd made sure she was too busy with study and work and establishing her career to think about him or the shipwrecked marriage—or to want the turmoil of falling in love again.

The thought that she'd clung to the legalities of her marriage because some remote part of her still wanted West made her go still inside, but she refused to yield to the possibility. She wasn't that needy.

West still affected her, she was big enough to admit that, but any woman with red blood pumping through her veins would find it hard to ignore him.

She stepped out of her office and pulled the door closed behind her. Stop thinking about him.

There was absolutely no point. Like the jades and artifacts she worked with, Gabriel West was past history—*way* in the past. She had wanted forever, and he hadn't. End of story. Getting close to West had been beyond what she could achieve. She simply hadn't had what it took to unlock whatever had passed for his heart.

She strolled slowly along the deserted, darkened corridor, shoes sinking into thick soft carpet as she passed the open double doors to one of the main display rooms. The musical ripple of water from a fountain almost masked the faint click of a door closing.

She froze. A chill swept down her spine. Someone was in the building with her.

Gently, she opened her briefcase, extracted her cell phone and pressed the short dial that would put her through to the night watchman. No alarms had gone off, the security system hadn't been breached, but that didn't mean safety. The stolen artifacts had disappeared without one alarm being tripped.

It could be the night watchman, or a staff member working late, as she was. The auction house was huge, and dealt in art, antiques and estate jewelry as well as Asian and Pacific-Rim artifacts. A number of Laine's staff had clearance to be in the building, although after the theft had been discovered three days ago they'd clamped down on security, and most of the keys had been handed in and security clearances revoked.

Before the call could be picked up, the night

watchman, Charlie Watson, stepped through a side door.

"Everything all right, Miss Laine?"

Tyler let out a breath and disconnected the call. "I heard a noise and got spooked. I was just ringing you to check if there was anyone else in the building."

Charlie's gaze lacked its usual warmth and slid away too quickly. "It was probably Mr. Laine you heard. He just left."

Mr. Laine. Last week Charlie would have referred to her adoptive brother as Richard. Tyler's stomach tightened at the loss of Charlie's easy manner. Everyone at Laine's was on edge; the police investigation and the intense media speculation had seen to that. But now that the first shock of the theft had passed, an uncomfortable speculation had set in—the kind of speculation Tyler should have been prepared for.

She had worked hard for Laine's—she'd worked even harder to be a part of her family—but there was no getting past the fact that she had been adopted into the wealthy jeweler family, not born into it. Pretty clothes and an exclusive education aside, she was the cuckoo in Laine's nest, with a murky past the media had latched on to like a starving dog closing its jaws on a juicy bone. She didn't need it spelled out that Charlie, who had always gone out of his way to be pleasant to her before, thought it was more than likely that she had had something to do with the theft.

He strolled past her into the display room. "Guess we're all a little jumpy since the theft."

He cast his eye over a glassed-in display of ivory that Tyler had catalogued and put together just before the jade had disappeared from a vault that had ten-inch steel walls, twenty-four-hour computer and camera surveillance, and a time lock that sealed it shut from five-thirty at night until eight in the morning.

A wave of weariness washed through Tyler as she slipped the cell phone back into her briefcase. "What do you think of the ivory?"

Charlie shoved his hands in his pockets and stared assessingly at the exquisitely carved set of Indonesian amulets. His gaze studiously avoided hers. "Not as pretty as the jade."

In Tyler's mind, as outwardly plain and workmanlike as the jade was, nothing was as "pretty."

When she'd first held the scabbard accoutrement she'd been filled with an inexplicable excitement that had gone beyond the thrill of finding artifacts that had been made and used by people not just centuries ago, but milleniums. Her palms had tingled, and heat had swept through her. She'd lost long minutes while she'd sat, the piece held loosely cupped in the palms of her hands—her mind oddly disconnected. It had taken the persistent buzz of the phone on her desk to pull her back to the present, and even then the subtle, tingling flow had continued, as if the crystalline grains contained within their cool green matrix the fiery imprint of life. The belt ornament and the carved bird had both felt similar, but neither was as powerful as the scabbard accoutrement, which was a warrior's piece, worn thin with time—smooth and uncomplicated—designed to encircle the sheath of a sword and proclaim, in this instance, not the warlord the warrior fought for, but his faith.

It was possible the warrior had either been a warlord himself, with no further insignia other than the solar symbol required, or he could have been one of the early warrior monks, predating the Shaolin.

The mystery of who had owned and used the jade, and how Chinese artifacts had come to be entombed in a Maori burial cave aside, the pieces had grabbed her at a deeper level than any other artifacts ever had. She'd experienced moments of connection with other objects before, as if the artifact in some strange way held the essence of a different time or place, or even a person, but never as strongly as this.

When the jade had been stolen, she'd felt a sense of violation out of all proportion to what she should have felt—as if the thief had walked into her home and taken a very private possession.

Despite the fact that her only link with the jade was a purely business one, and that the possession of the pieces was open to public debate, in a strange way, on a very personal level, the jade *had* belonged to her.

Fifteen minutes later, Tyler drove into the underground entrance of her apartment building, escaping the leading edge of a tropical storm front that had swept down from the north.

She parked in her space, gathered her briefcase, and locked the car, shivering as a damp blast of air tugged at her lightweight jacket and skirt, and frowning because the garage was close to pitch-black. Several of the lights must have died at once, or else the storm had knocked them out, leaving only the lights above the elevator and those in the stairwell shining.

Thunder rumbled and a flicker of lightning briefly lit the gloom as she walked toward the stairwell. Her apartment was on the ground floor—a luxury she'd been happy to afford for herself because the gardens around the apartment block were so beautiful. When she came home from work, she liked nothing better than to sit out on her tiny sun-drenched terrace, surrounded by cool, glossy green rhododendrons and nikau palms and fall asleep on her lounger reading a book.

A footfall registered, out of sync with hers. She paused to listen, but almost instantly shook off the paranoia that gripped her. No other vehicle had entered the garage since she'd arrived. What she'd heard had probably been an echo of her own step bouncing off the concrete walls.

Lately, she'd been jumping at her own shadow. A few odd things had happened, including several phone calls from someone who'd hung up as soon as she'd answered. On a couple of occasions she'd been certain that she'd been followed, even though she hadn't so much as caught a glimpse of anyone.

Another footfall sounded, this time sharply distinct. A raw flash of alarm went through her and her step quickened. She threw an assessing glance around the gloomy cavern of the garage.

A hand snaked out of darkness and closed on her arm, wrenching her to a halt. Adrenaline flooded her system, almost stopping her heart. Her arm jerked in automatic reflex as she spun, teeth bared, and stepped into her attacker, throwing him off balance as she snapped her elbow into a face that was eerily blanked out by a balaclava. He grunted with pain and released his hold. A second man materialized out of the smothering blackness and ripped the briefcase from her.

Fear and rage and the sharp instincts of a child who'd spent more time defending herself than she'd ever spent with tea sets or dolls burst hotly through her. With her right hand now free, she swung, fingers bunched into a tight fist, and connected with the solid bone of a jaw, snapping her attacker's head back. A strangled sound burst from his mouth, and the balaclava was knocked askew, giving her a glimpse of dark skin and high, slanted cheekbones as she wheeled, holding her handbag to her chest so that there was nothing trailing for either man to grab, and flung herself toward the elevator.

A hand snagged at her jacket. Gritting her teeth, she wrenched free. Hair spilled around her face, half blinding her, and in that moment the doors of the elevator slid open. Relief flooded her as light flared across the bare expanse of concrete, spotlighting her in its beam so that she felt like a rabbit caught in the glare of headlights. West's startled gaze locked with hers, then white light exploded in her head.

Chapter 3

West reached Tyler a split second after she crumpled.

After the initial kick of surprise, he was rock steady, breathing controlled. His mind shifted smoothly through his options, the change from civilian to soldier instantaneous.

Aside from the light pouring from the elevator and the stairwell, the car park was abnormally dark. Someone had knocked the lights out, which meant that the attack was planned. West eased forward to crouch over Tyler, at the same time straining to listen, to get some idea of the direction in which the two men had gone, but the rumble of the storm and the heavy drumbeat of rain effectively muffled sound.

A faint scrape of metal on metal jerked West's head around. He probed the silent reaches of the underground car park, systematically examining the ranks of vehicles, his mind loose, open to peripheral data he might otherwise miss, open to that other sense that was as much a part of him as breathing. An icy calmness gripped him like a cold hand at his nape. The men who had attacked Tyler were still here.

A flash of movement drew his eye. The cough of a car starting bounced off the walls, and lights swept the gloom as the vehicle spun and accelerated toward the exit. Abruptly, the roar of the engine cut out as the car took the ramp up onto the street.

West switched his attention back to Tyler. A disorienting sense of déjà vu transported him back to a night one month ago and the disastrous meet with Renwick.

She was lying on her side, still and painfully exposed in the wash of light from the elevator, tawny hair a silky pool around her face, the short skirt of her tailored suit revealing a tanned length of elegant leg that made her seem both exotic and fragile against the grim crudity of the underground car park.

At first glance he couldn't see any blood. West gently turned her on her back, as he searched for the wound. His heart slammed in his chest when he found the goose egg on the side of her head and felt the dampness of blood.

''West?'' Tyler blinked, and lifted a hand to shield

her eyes from the multi-hued glare of light that shifted across her vision. She felt sluggish and sick, and her head felt strange—hot and cold, and prickling—and she was having trouble focusing. There were two of West, and in her opinion, one had always been more than enough.

The chill of the dusty concrete struck through the crumpled cotton of her suit, making her shiver. Awkwardly, she pushed herself into a sitting position, ignoring his sharp demand that she stay where she was. She needed to get up, get moving.

Her mind flinched from the fact that she'd been hit on the head, but there was no other explanation for her to be lying on the garage floor. Her right hand was numb, and her arm and shoulder hurt, but she managed to wobble onto her knees. She heard West's soft curse, then his hands closed on her arms, steadying her, and she didn't complain because she was having trouble orienting herself at all.

He cupped her chin, his fingers startlingly hot against her skin, and abruptly his face snapped into focus.

He stared intently into her eyes. "What's your name?"

Bemused, Tyler answered.

"Today's date?"

Pinpointing the date was more difficult, but that was mostly because she hadn't paid much attention to dates lately. She repeated the date. "I don't have any memory loss."

As disoriented as she felt, she knew she'd been mugged and knocked out. The sequence of events was burned into her mind like a series of freeze frames. She could remember the moment her briefcase had been wrenched from her grip, the flash of light when she'd been hit.

A car swept into the underground garage and she tensed, her breath coming in sharply.

"Don't hit me," West murmured, and for the first time she focused directly on his face: hot gold eyes, tanned olive skin, black hair tumbled and loose around his shoulders—the glitter of a silver stud in his ear.

He looked as if he'd just rolled out of bed, sleepy and unkempt, as alert as a cat, and through the throbbing whirl of nausea and exhaustion she wondered—and not for the first time—if he slept alone.

Something grabbed in her throat, her heart, a hot pulse of emotion that shook her to the core.

Hit West? Now there was a fantasy.... She just needed her head to stop spinning first.

His fingers closed warmly around her clenched fist, making her aware of the numbing ache in her knuckles, the symphony of pain that stretched from her fingertips all the way to her shoulder, skipping her face, then throbbing somewhere deep in her skull.

"Let me see," he demanded softly. "Open your hand."

For the craziest moment she thought he'd said, "Open your heart."

She couldn't help the bemused smile that twitched at her lips. The pain aside, she felt ridiculous—giddy—like a drunk on a bender. "Last time I heard, you weren't a medical doctor."

His mouth curved in a quick, hard smile. "I've been called a lot of names, but never that."

Reluctantly, she uncurled her fingers. God, she hated it when she got hurt—hated to look at the damage. She heard his rough intake of breath.

"Oh, jeez, you belted him. Where in hell did you learn to hit like that?"

She ignored his question in favor of surveying her swollen knuckles, and the grazes decorating them. "I broke his jaw," she said with satisfaction. "I felt it go."

"Are you hurt anywhere else?"

She glanced around and saw her handbag lying beside her. With an effort of will, she snagged the strap. At least she still had her credit cards and her driver's license, and they hadn't gotten her car keys. "Yeah, in my heart. They took my laptop. The bastards took my laptop."

She thought he said, "When did you get so tough?" then a wave of dizziness caught her.

She leaned into his shoulder and gulped down a deep breath, which didn't do much to alleviate the dizziness or the pain, then wound an arm around his neck, searching for the leverage to get to her feet. It struck her that in the last five years West had never been so useful.

She pushed against his shoulder, but a warm palm cupped her nape, effectively holding her in place and making her feel as weak as a day-old kitten.

"Don't you ever give up? *Stay still.* You've got a head wound and you're bleeding. I'm going to check you out a bit more, then get you to a hospital."

"I'm not going to a hospital. I hate hospitals."

"That's one thing we've got in common."

As he shrugged out of his leather jacket and draped it around her shoulders, swamping her in heavy, soft warmth, the rich scent of leather, she worried at the oddness of the terse comment. As far as she was concerned the only thing they actually had in common was a marriage certificate. Blinking, she resisted the urge to let her forehead rest on his shoulder again, or even worse, snuggle into the curve of his neck. She wasn't a leaner—she couldn't remember the last time she'd leaned on anyone—but right now the temptation was almost too much. She'd been exhausted before the attack; now she felt as though she was swimming through molasses. "I feel…strange—"

"Stay awake."

She felt his fingers moving gently over her scalp. He found a tender spot and she winced.

His breath stirred in her hair. "Oh yeah, he hit you good. You've got a lump, and a cut that's going to need stitching. Go to sleep and I'll tan your hide."

The unexpected humor would have made her smile if she hadn't felt so startled and so sick.

"Promises," she muttered, then everything receded, slipping into blackness again.

A hoarse curse scraped from West's throat as Tyler sagged into his chest. He caught her hard against him, lowered her to the concrete, then on another soft curse, jerked his T-shirt over his head, tore a strip of white interlock off and bandaged the seeping cut on the side of her head. When he lifted her into his arms, her head lolled against his shoulder and fear shafted through him. Head wounds were dicey things, she'd wake up with the mother of all headaches at the very least. He refused to think about other possibilities.

Seconds later he strapped Tyler into the passenger seat of his car, slid behind the wheel and searched one-handed for his cell phone as he took the ramp out of the underground garage.

He found the phone, pressed the emergency code, and waited for the operator to put him through to Accident and Emergency. When the hospital had all the details, he settled down to driving, the damp night air chill on his bare skin as he shoved the car through traffic. Rain continued to stream down in a light, steady drizzle that rose up off the slick streets as a thin mist, wreathing the fast-moving, raucous flow of inner-city traffic.

West's heart was pounding, his belly tight with apprehension. He felt savage, wary and electrified by what had just happened. His mind fastened on the moment when the elevator doors had opened and Tyler's dark gaze had found his, hooked somewhere deep inside him and clung. That moment had almost stopped his heart.

He'd moved into the apartment in Tyler's building with the specific purpose of getting close to his wife, but a part of him hadn't believed Tyler would ever allow him close again.

Just minutes ago she'd all but crawled inside his skin.

The lights ahead flashed red. He swore beneath his breath, considered running the light, then braked.

The abrupt jolting motion sent a shaft of pain through Tyler's head. She winced and opened her eyes, for a moment disoriented by the glare of lights off rain-slick roads, and West sitting beside her, his torso bare. The last thing she remembered she'd been kneeling on cold concrete, leaning on West, and he'd been wearing a T-shirt.

The lights changed. West accelerated and, gingerly, she straightened, keeping her head as still as possible. The second she moved, she felt the touch of West's gaze as powerfully as if he'd reached out and physically touched her. "How long have I been out?"

"Five minutes. We'll be at the hospital in two. And don't argue. Aside from needing stitches you've probably got a concussion."

"That's a safe bet." Her head throbbed with a deep, frightening ache and she was seeing colors. That was the clincher. The only other time she could remember seeing colors had been when she'd been thrown from a horse at age thirteen, without the benefit of a protective helmet.

West turned into a car-park entrance and pulled into a space. Tyler recognized the A&E entrance of Auckland Hospital.

She reached up to touch the bandage that was wound around her head, and somehow managed to misjudge the distance so that her fingers connected with her head more violently than she'd intended. Hot pain flashed through her skull, and her stomach rolled.

She sucked in a shallow breath, then another, and groped for the door handle. "I'm going to be sick."

Instead of the door releasing she must have hit the window button because glass slid down and damp air flowed across her face. She heard a soft imprecation. Seconds later her door swung open and West leaned in, released her seat belt, and she found herself hauled out into the rain. His arms came around her as her stomach cramped painfully, anchoring her against him as she emptied the meagre contents of her stomach into the shrubbery bordering the car park.

When she was finished she sagged against him, uncaring that it was raining and that they were both getting wet. An odd peacefulness settled over her at his silent support, his heat and strength engulfing her. All of the issues that existed between them aside, she was too needy, in too much pain, and too disoriented to do anything but accept his help.

The thought drifted into her mind that West might have broken her heart, but he had never broken her trust.

As crazy as it seemed, it was true. He had made promises, and he had kept them, and she'd married him knowing that their relationship would be constantly sidelined by SAS operations. If she was honest, in that sense, she had let him down.

A car cruised past. The bright gleam of headlights scythed the drizzle and broke the fragile peace.

"Are you ready to make a move?" West's voice was low, with that calm note that said he would stay here holding her in the rain if that was what she wanted.

She'd forgotten that about him—that still, quiet quality. Years ago it had intrigued her. She'd fallen in love with his dark, soft voice, but somewhere along the way, the very qualities that had drawn her so powerfully had started to grate.

He had been too controlled, too patient, and she hadn't had enough of either quality.

"Can you walk?" His voice was close to her ear.

"Just."

He left her leaning against the car while he closed the window and collected her bag and the leather jacket. She heard the gentle thunk of locks engaging, then he draped the jacket over her shoulders, wrapped his arm around her waist and urged her toward the brightly lit entrance of A&E.

The rain eased off as they approached the steps,

leaving the night still and sodden and heavy with the scents of car exhaust and bitumen.

Tyler lifted her head and caught her reflection in the glass doors, then wished she hadn't. Her face was as white as the makeshift bandage around her head; her hair was straggling around her shoulders and what she could see of her suit beneath the jacket was wrinkled and sticking clammily to her skin.

West, in stark contrast, looked fresh and sharp and gorgeous, his bronzed shoulders sleek and glistening under the lights. The fact that he had no shirt didn't seem to affect him. "You know, West, I had this fantasy of how in control I'd be the next time I bumped into you. This isn't it."

"Tell me about it." He paused on the steps and produced a clean handkerchief so she could wipe her face.

Groggy as she was, she noticed it was monogrammed. "You get your handkerchiefs monogrammed?"

"Don't crucify me over it. They were a gift from a friend." An offbeat smile flitted across his mouth. "Roma McCabe gives them to me at Christmas just to tick me off."

The humor in his voice, the sheer intimacy of the gift threw Tyler off balance. Numbly, she wiped her face and blew her nose. She knew who Roma McCabe was—the only daughter of the wealthy and powerful Lombard family. She was also aware of West's business connections with that family, and that Roma had married one of West's friends, Ben McCabe, but somehow the closeness of the connection had never sunk in. She had always considered West to be a loner—a man no one could ever truly get close to—most especially not a woman.

It registered that despite having lived with West for three years, she didn't know him at all.

It also registered that against all the odds she was jealous.

The wail of an arriving ambulance went through West like a knife as the doors to the brightly lit waiting room slid open, flooding his nostrils with the smells of antiseptics and cleaners, the stale miasma of too many people. The abrupt sensory overload briefly spun him back to his childhood and early teens, to broken ribs and pain and, once, the wrong end of a knife. The proximity of sick, hurt people—the hospital itself—closed around him, made the back of his throat tighten. He dipped and nuzzled the top of Tyler's head, breathed in her pretty, subtle scents, at once taking refuge in the woman in his arms, and conferring protection. If he'd had any doubts before about walking back into Tyler's life, they were gone.

She might not like it, but right now, she needed him.

Chapter 4

Late-morning sunlight angled through Tyler's hospital-room window, flooding the crowded room with a brilliance that made her wince as she straightened from gathering her clothes and shoes from the small bedside locker. With careful movements, she transferred the items into the small overnight bag that was lying open on her bed.

Apart from Detective Farrell and her father's personal assistant, Claire Wheeler, the room was full of men: her father, Harrison, and her brother, Richard, Ray Cornell, the investigating detective, and two of Laine's key managers, Kyle Montgomery and Ashley James.

They were all here ostensibly out of concern for her welfare, but Tyler couldn't help a spurt of cynicism at that thought. Over the past few days, after the initial storm of publicity over the theft, she'd noticed her work colleagues had begun to avoid her, and the sense of isolation stung.

Unless the business managers of Laine's diamond house could shed light on the theft or the mugging, there wasn't much point to the visit. With the press crucifying her for the loss of the jade, and the details of her past splashed across the front pages of all the major dailies, there was nothing much to do but pick over the carcass.

The media had dismissed her doctorate, her years of experience and her charity work. They had thrown a murky shadow over the fact that she was even in the business of buying, selling and consulting on rare jade and artifacts. They had taught the public and, it seemed, her work colleagues, to view her in a different light. She was no longer Dr. Tyler Laine, expert on Eastern and Pacific-Rim artifacts, she was the daughter of Sonny Mullane, a petty criminal with a record as long as both of his lean, sinewy arms. Aside from operating as a small-time fence, Sonny had been a thief, a safecracker, and a pimp. If there was any crime he hadn't committed other than murder, then, as far as Tyler was concerned, that crime hadn't yet been invented.

According to the tabloids, the fact that Sonny Mullane's daughter had been adopted by the Laine family didn't make her any better than she had been.

"Can you remember any other details about the people who attacked you?"

Tyler shifted her attention to Cornell. The question was delivered politely, but with a flat patience that told Tyler that no matter how devoid of emotion his light gray eyes appeared to be, Cornell wanted more from her than the scanty details she'd so far been able to supply him.

"I can't give you any more of a description," she said flatly. "There were two of them. It was dark and they were wearing balaclavas. One of them was olive-skinned and tanned: he looked Asian."

She gripped the bedside table and lowered herself enough that she could perch on the edge of the bed. Just those simple actions were enough to make her break out in a sweat. She'd protested at spending the night in hospital, but there was no getting past the fact that her head was still throbbing despite the painkillers she'd taken, and that she was still wobbly on her feet.

Aside from the initial head injury, and the damage she'd done to her right hand and shoulder when she'd thrown that punch, she'd sustained a second head injury when she'd fallen and hit her head on the concrete. The first hit had been brutal enough to concuss her; the second one hadn't been as violent, but had compounded the first injury with the added bruising and swelling. On top of all that, she was bruised and stiff all down her left side from the fall.

Gingerly, she pushed hair away from her face.

She'd managed to shower that morning and change into the jeans and cotton shirt Harrison had brought in, but her hair was still a mess, tangled and matted around the wound, and she'd left it that way. Her one attempt to drag a comb through the tangles had left her clinging to the bathroom counter, a fine film of perspiration beading her upper lip.

The doctor who'd treated her the previous evening had only needed two stitches to close the cut on her head, but the area was still swollen, her scalp so tight and sensitive that even the movement of her hair hurt.

Some time around midnight, she'd stopped seeing colors. In medical terms, the swelling in her brain had subsided to a point where it was no longer pressing on the optic nerves, thus producing the neon-bright display, but she still felt oversensitive and fragile. Colors were too bright, voices were too loud—even the surface of her skin felt oversensitive, as if several layers had been peeled away and all of her nerve endings exposed.

"You said you thought someone followed you on two separate occasions the previous week. Have you got any idea who that might have been?"

The question was clipped and businesslike, not Cornell this time, but his partner, Elaine Farrell.

Tyler lifted her chin, and spoke carefully, mostly because the answer was so obvious, but partly because the small movements of her mouth and jaw pulled at the skin of her scalp and intensified the deep ache, so that even talking hurt. ''If I'd been absolutely certain that I was being followed, and had any idea who was following me I would have done something about it.''

The small buzz of conversation in the room stopped.

Cornell went down on his haunches, his gaze neutral. ''Are you certain the dark-skinned man who attacked you was Chinese?''

Anger flickered at Cornell's deliberate alteration of the facts, his subtle sidestep into the shady realms of the jade investigation. There had been some speculation that the Chinese interests could be included in the thefts, but that was mostly media generated. ''I saw part of his face. I'm certain he was *Asian,* not that he was Chinese.''

Richard made a sound of disbelief. ''Are you saying the mugging could be linked with the theft of the jade?''

Cornell didn't acknowledge Richard's question, or answer. All of his attention remained focused on Tyler—the pressure of his gaze like a weight.

Bitterness and an odd indifference congealed in Tyler's stomach—a grim remnant from childhood. Cornell was questioning her in order to track down the men who'd assaulted her, but she was beginning to feel more like the offender than the victim. She could feel herself stepping back inside, divorcing herself from the legal process that was unfolding around her.

With an effort of will, she slammed the door on the temptation to simply close off and go blank. When she'd been a child she'd been an expert at the tactics—the ice-queen of eight-year-olds. She'd worked hard to leave that pattern behind; it had taken years, and she'd be damned if she would start running now. There was too much at stake, too much to lose. Her reputation, her career. Her family.

She glanced at Richard and Harrison. They were standing side-by-side—both tall, lean and tanned, with light brown hair. Except for the thirty years Harrison had on Richard and the silvery wings at his temples, the likeness was so pronounced that they could have been brothers. Their jaws were both identically set, their dark eyes cold, voices clipped, as they grilled Cornell about the possibility of a connection between the mugging and the jade theft, and for a moment, confusion and an acute sense of separation swamped Tyler. It was obvious that Harrison and Richard were father and son—also obvious that they were similar in ways that transcended the father/son relationship.

They were her family, but in subtle ways they weren't. Harrison's wife, Louisa, had always been the glue that had held them all together, but since her death three years before, Tyler had felt herself drifting, her connection to both Harrison and Richard increasingly more tenuous.

Richard crossed his arms over his chest, his frustration palpable. ''So what the hell *are* we investigating? A theft, or some kind of conspiracy?''

With her as the prime suspect.

Tyler rubbed at her temples. Her mind was still fuzzy, her head throbbing despite the painkillers she'd had with breakfast. ''Leave it, Richard. The guy was Asian, that's a fact. I was mugged, that's another fact. At this point there is nothing to connect the mugging with the theft of the jade. As for the phone calls, and being followed…'' Her own frustration welled, sending a fresh stab of pain through her skull. ''All of that started happening *before* the robbery, so how could any of it possibly be connected?''

She could feel the consensus of opinion. The theft of the jade had sent shock waves through the world of artifacts. The mystery of who had taken the jade, and *how* it had been stolen, when to all intents and purposes Laine's security system had not been breached, was disturbing enough. No one wanted to believe that the theft could be more complicated than simple larceny.

But if she was cynical enough, and right now it was hard to be anything but cynical, the police, and everyone present in the room, had to be examining the possibility that she was using last night's incident to implicate the Chinese in the jade theft. The jade was, after all, Chinese in origin.

Although why would anyone, let alone Chinese people, attack her when they already had the jade?

A renegade bubble of humor surfaced. Unless, of course, she had somehow stumbled onto the set of a "B" grade movie, and the bad guys wanted to cut her out of the money, bump her off and dump her body.

Abruptly, the implications were too much—especially if the press decided there was a connection.

She met Richard's gaze coolly. "If I had any idea who it is that's been following me and doing the heavy-breathing routine over the phone, I would have tracked him down and dealt with him the same way I dealt with the guy last night."

Richard looked momentarily perplexed.

Cornell rose to his feet and slipped his notebook in his briefcase. "She broke his jaw."

The moment when she'd swung that punch replayed through Tyler's mind. She hadn't made a conscious decision to hit him—that punch had burst from deep inside and she couldn't have pulled it if she'd tried. Even now, just thinking about it made the fury well up and sent adrenaline pumping through her veins.

"You broke his jaw?"

The question was soft, clipped. Harrison.

She had never called her adoptive father Dad, and he had never asked her to—by the time the Laine family had adopted her she had been eight going on thirty. She and Harrison had compromised with his first name.

She met his dark gaze. Surprise jolted her when

she saw tenderness there. She let out a breath. "I felt the bone give."

There was an odd silence as the new tidbit of information was digested. It was the kind of blank silence she hadn't faced since she was eight and Louisa had found her food stash moldering in her closet, along with the wad of money she'd accumulated from selling the clothes and shoes she'd been showered with and didn't need—which had amounted to most of them. In the world she'd come from, cash was more important than a Barbie doll wardrobe.

Harrison nodded, as if it was a perfectly normal occurrence that his daughter should break a mugger's jaw.

"Could the other offender have been female?"

The voice was husky, female. Tyler met Farrell's gaze. For a split second she wondered if Farrell was playing with subtleties and trying for a guilt reaction that might connect her to both crimes, then the no-nonsense tone in her voice registered. Cornell was working the tactics; Farrell was simply being thorough. It was a valid question—plenty of women committed crimes—and Farrell hadn't etched out a career in a hard-ass, male-dominated profession by pussyfooting around unpopular issues.

She saw again the flash of a male jaw and slanted cheekbone, felt the steely grip on her arm. A memory surfaced. "They smelled male."

She caught the instant respect in Farrell's eyes, felt the recoil that went around the room.

Amusement caught her off balance again. So, okay, noticing the scent of the people attacking her might not be a habit cultivated in the best circles, but she *had* smelled them, and it was a relief to remember something else definitive when the attack had happened in a blur of shadows and adrenaline.

"They were both male," a dark, cool voice affirmed. "That piece of information was in the statements we both gave last night."

Tyler's head jerked up. She winced, her eyes squeezed closed, but not before she'd glimpsed West leaning against the doorjamb, wearing jeans and a white T-shirt, a sleek black jacket hugging his shoulders.

West's gaze briefly touched on each of the people filling Tyler's room. Anger stirred through him at the inquisition that was taking place. He knew the police had a job to do, but her family could damn well back off. Tyler was tough, a real fighter, but she was tired and practically crawling out of her skin with pain.

He didn't know what time she had got to sleep last night, but it had been ten-thirty before a doctor had been free to stitch the cut on her head, and after midnight before the statements had been completed. West had left the hospital at around one-thirty, after Tyler had been settled in her room.

"Who in hell are you?"

West ignored the GQ mannequin asking the question. He knew a number of the people in the room: Ray Cornell and Elaine Farrell, Richard and Harrison. He recognized Ashley James, who had been Richard's right-hand man forever, but the woman and the suit with the question were strangers. They weren't cops, that was obvious. They were too manicured—too nervy—which meant they had to be two of Harrison's newer employees.

Ray Cornell nodded briefly. "West."

Amusement at Cornell's wariness took the edge off West's growing fury. "It's been a while."

West bumped into Cornell occasionally. Ray was ex-SAS, now a detective at Auckland Central. The most recent occasion they'd hooked up had been a year ago when West's friend Ben McCabe had been shot at, and they'd spent a couple of hours at Central giving statements.

Harrison acknowledged West, as he always did, with neutrality and politeness.

As out of place with the Laine family as he'd always been, West had never felt antagonism from his father-in-law, simply a void that had shown no sign of diminishing. The gap in life experience had just been too broad for either of them to breach. Richard, on the other hand, had no problem with the void; his cold gaze said just how much he liked it, and the bigger the better. West had never had a problem with his brother-in-law's attitude, except that it had always hurt Tyler.

West had few people in his life he had ever been

able to care for, but his feelings were clean-cut and simple: he would die for them. The way he'd grown up had narrowed his perceptions to absolutes, leaving him with a bedrock that alienated most people. The way he was wasn't easy or comfortable, but his friends understood him.

West's gaze touched on Tyler's tangled hair, her utter stillness claiming his attention. As hard as he'd tried to make Tyler understand how he felt, *how he was inside,* how difficult it was for him to change and adjust, she hadn't wanted to listen.

Harrison softly ordered his people from the room. As James, the pretty lady executive and the suit, who answered to the name of Kyle, filed past him, relief loosened some of West's tension.

He wanted these people out of here, ASAP, and he wanted Tyler out, too. When he'd arrived the press had been gathering downstairs. Maybe they weren't hunting for Tyler, but he wouldn't place any bets on it.

Farrell offered him a hand, her gaze speculative.

West recognized the look, and the curiosity. Down under, the military world meshed closely enough with civilian forces that the gossip spread. A number of Auckland detectives were ex-SAS. It was a recognized career path for military personnel to slide sideways into civilian law enforcement. A lot of them ended up on the Special Tactics Squad, or the AOS, the Armed Offenders Squad. He also knew that

Farrell was one of the few women who had served on the AOS, and that she was a current member. She would know he'd resigned from the SAS, and why.

Farrell lifted a brow. ''Heard you turned to the dark side.''

''Private enterprise pays more than the military.''

Cornell snapped his briefcase closed. ''How long have you been out?''

West glanced at Tyler as she zipped her overnight bag closed and straightened. ''Three weeks, give or take a day,'' but his mind wasn't on conversation.

Tyler's face was white, her gaze glassy. He recognized the way she was moving, the way she was feeling, because he'd been there a couple of times with head injuries. It was a good act, but he'd seen drunks with more coordination.

He stepped around Harrison and Richard. His fingers curled around the grip of the bag. ''I'll take that.''

Her gaze locked with his, shooting green fire. He logged her almost imperceptible flinch—as if the emotion, and the light, had hurt—felt her internal battle. Tyler had always been as independent and solitary as a cat despite the satin cushion of the Laines' wealth, and all the company that that money attracted.

Her fingers remained locked around the grip.

''Let me.''

He felt the moment when she gave in, and grimly acknowledged that this was how it was going to be.

He'd always known trying to get Tyler back would be tough—he just hadn't realized how tough.

For the past few days, he'd made it his business to be where she was around the apartment complex whenever possible. It hadn't been easy because she'd been working long hours, and each time she'd simply walked past him, barely making eye contact. The only break he'd had had been when he'd stepped out of the elevator while she was being attacked.

Right now, Tyler needed his help, and he was ruthlessly using every advantage that came his way, but she was making it more than clear that while she did need help, she didn't need *him*.

Brilliant light flashed through the room, followed by the motorized whirr of a camera.

West caught a glimpse of a dark-clad shoulder as the photographer slid through the door, and cursed beneath his breath. He made eye contact with Cornell, who was looking pissed. "When I walked through reception there were reporters camped there, plus a TV crew."

Cornell swore. West knew that Ray had coped with his share of media attention over the years, and some of it hadn't enhanced his career.

Cornell strode to the door with Farrell following in his wake. "I'll hold them for five, but you owe me."

West jerked his head in a street gesture that drew a quick hard grin from Cornell. "Always."

A question was shot at Tyler—the same photographer trying his luck again.

West caught the cold register of Cornell's voice, then footsteps pounding down the hospital corridor.

His hand settled at the small of Tyler's back. "I'm taking you out of here. Now. And don't even think about it," he countered flatly, before she could argue. "The hospital's not handing out your room number, but one reporter made it in here. It won't be long before the rest find you. Cornell's running interference, but he won't be able to hold them for long."

Chapter 5

The horror of the press and a TV crew waiting to descend on her made Tyler go cold inside.

She caught the end of a sharp exchange between Richard and a member of the hospital staff about how, exactly, the press had managed to find her room—saw the strain on Harrison's face, and abruptly, her decision was made.

Her family had been through hell and back with the theft of the jade. The media circus had just begun to die down, but now, with this latest attack on her, the situation had gone from zero to crazy again.

There was no way, if she could help it, that she wanted Harrison and Richard caught in the spotlight with her.

She picked up her bag, slung the strap over her

shoulder and met West's gaze. He had helped her last night, but that had been an emergency situation. She didn't know why he was here now; still, she recognized a rescue when she saw one. "I wasn't about to argue."

Richard fell into step with them as they walked toward the bank of elevators. He was making no bones about the fact that he didn't like West taking her home, but over the years, Tyler had gotten used to his subtle air of disapproval. She'd been eight when the welfare people had driven her to the Laine home and she'd been ushered into a TV room where Richard had been watching a documentary. Back then, he'd been a lean, gangling fourteen-year-old—tall and intimidating—and too close to adult for her to easily trust.

They'd both been wary of the abrupt change and, somehow, despite the passage of years, that wariness had never quite faded.

Tyler was relieved to see that only Harrison and Claire were waiting there; everyone else had left.

Richard cast her a shuttered look. "I thought you were going to Dad's place."

"I don't need nursing, just a good night's sleep, and I'd rather be in my own bed. And this way you and Dad can avoid the press. Besides..."

She took another measured breath and let it out slowly. She didn't want to say what she was about to say, but she'd kept it secret long enough, and it wasn't a secret, it was just... Resignation, and a small rill of amusement surfaced, for a moment pushing back her cacophony of aches and pains—Harrison and Richard would throw a fit. Talk about the clap of doom. "West lives in my building."

"He *what*—"

"Don't start." Exasperation sparked along with affection. Somehow Richard always made her feel as irresponsible as a teenager. Only six years separated them, but it could have been sixty. Some days she could swear he was older than Harrison. Eight years ago, he'd taken it upon himself to warn her against marrying West. When the marriage had folded, he'd had the grace not to say anything, but his careful silence had conveyed his view. He'd never approved of West, period.

His jaw tightened. "I don't like it. You were attacked in your building. It's supposed to be a secure complex, but it's obviously—"

"I was *mugged*—in the car park. They got my laptop. I don't think lightning's likely to strike twice."

They came to a halt in front of the elevator doors. West's hand was still resting lightly at the small of her back, but she wasn't complaining. She felt steadier than she had earlier, but her head still felt as though it was on a gimbal, and her sense of balance was shaky. Right now she needed the support.

Richard looked like he had a lot more to say, but he confined himself to a hard stare in West's direction.

West jerked his head in the direction of an elevator farther down the corridor. "Not that one. We're taking the service elevator."

Tyler suppressed a smile as they traversed a short stretch of corridor to a small alcove that concealed a battered elevator. This was a first for Harrison and Richard. They were taking the back way out.

She let out a relieved breath when the steel doors finally slid closed, and the elevator started its descent.

There was another reason she wanted West to be the one to drive her home, and she'd avoided it for long enough: it was time they had a confrontation. She wasn't ready for a fight—*she wasn't well enough for a fight*—but she needed to find out why, with all of the properties and apartment complexes available in Auckland City, he had chosen hers.

Outside the sun struck down, bouncing off light masonry walls, and glittering off cars. After the comparative coolness of the hospital, it was like walking into a blast furnace.

Tyler groped in her bag, found her sunglasses and slipped them onto the bridge of her nose. The relief of the soothing dimness, and the sense of being able to retreat behind the anonymity of dark lenses, went through her with a small shudder. All of her life, she'd valued her privacy and her independence, and she'd fought fiercely for both. She'd had enough of being on the back foot, and she had absolutely had enough of notoriety.

Harrison, Claire and Richard turned in the direction of the public car park. Instead of following, West guided her across an open area of asphalt, which was filled with free bays and designated spaces. She noticed he'd also slipped on dark glasses and had removed his jacket and was carrying it slung over one arm. He didn't say anything, but his silence wasn't tense, and she was reminded of the previous evening, when he'd just held on to her and it had felt peaceful. Even now, despite the threat of the press he was completely unruffled, and letting her set the pace. They could have been tourists going for a casual stroll.

She noticed that instead of moving toward the public car park, they'd remained in the enclosed restricted zone, which was filled with freight bays and designated spaces. Several signs said Authorized Parking Only.

The fact that West had bypassed legitimate parking in favor of the restricted area that fed into the back entrance of the hospital had to have been deliberate. ''You knew we'd be coming out this way.''

''With the press here, it was the best option.''

That would also explain how he'd known where the service elevator was. He'd probably used the elevator when he'd come up to her room and got, not only her, but Harrison and Richard out from beneath the noses of the press. It had been a rescue mission from start to finish, carried out with military precision. He'd even sent Cornell down to defuse the situation with the press and buy them some time. She met his gaze, disconcerted at the lengths he'd gone to protect not only her, but her family, and the ease with which he'd done it. "Thanks."

"No problem. I should have got you out faster than I did."

When they reached his car he unlocked the doors, then walked around to the passenger side and opened hers before placing her overnight-bag and his jacket on the back seat.

She dropped her handbag onto the floor of the car, gripped the passenger-side door with her good hand, started to climb into the car, and stopped when the action of twisting, bending and dipping her head sent a hot pain stabbing from her neck all the way to the base of her spine. Sucking in a breath, Tyler braced herself once again on the door, and slowly eased herself into the passenger seat and pulled the door closed.

"What's wrong?"

"I feel like an old lady."

He grinned, the flash of his teeth startlingly white against his dark jaw. "With any luck, if you stop punching out bad guys, you'll live to be one. What *exactly* hurts?"

"Aside from my head and my hand? My neck just decided to freeze up, and my back hurts all the way down my right side. Even my big toe's aching."

Behind the shield of his dark glasses his gaze was enigmatic. "Sounds like you've pinched your sciatic nerve. When that happens all the muscles contract around the nerve, causing the stiffness. You probably did it when you swung that punch. What you need is some anti-inflammatory medication to take the swelling down.''

She reached for her seat belt, wincing as even that movement sent fire shooting down between her shoulder blades. ''The doctor checked my spine last night.''

''He wouldn't have picked up on the pinched nerve. It usually takes a few hours for the muscles to stiffen up.''

She twisted, attempting to fasten the belt, but the angle was awkward, the fingers of her right hand stiff and clumsy.

''I'll do that.'' West leaned over, took the belt clip from her and fastened it, and she was abruptly aware of him in a completely female way. He nodded toward a bright blue van with a TV station logo painted on the side that was nosing into the car park. ''Looks like they're going for the service elevator.''

West maneuvered out of the parking space and eased past the van which had pulled into a slot reserved for freight vehicles. A small shudder swept Tyler at just how close she'd come to being cornered by the press in her hospital room.

As they turned into traffic, Tyler settled back in her seat and forced tensed muscles to relax as she watched traffic slide by.

West picked up his cell phone and made a call, then glanced across at her. ''I can pick you up an anti-inflammatory in a few minutes. It's a prescription drug, but that's no problem. I've got a friend who'll prescribe over the phone."

As he drove, Tyler turned her attention to the car. She hadn't paid it much attention last night, but now the Saab was hard to ignore. It was black and sleek and expensive, the lines clean but subtle. She knew a little about cars. She'd done some research before she'd bought her own. For a long time she'd wavered between buying a Porsche or a Mercedes coupe, then sanity had prevailed. If she'd bought anything that pretty and that fast, she would have been dead in a week. As cautious and meticulous as she was in her everyday life, she had a streak of recklessness that showed itself when she drove. Harrison had wanted her to buy a BMW, and in the end she'd gone with that choice. With their heavy steel bodies, ABS braking systems and air bags, they were one of the closest things to an armoured vehicle a motorist could buy.

The only car reputed to be safer than a BMW was a Saab. It was a surprise to see West driving one.

"What is it?"

She blinked, the soft question after the peaceful silence startling. "I was admiring your car, and wondering why you didn't go for something with more muscle."

"I've got a four-wheel drive for hunting. That's enough muscle for me." He stopped for a set of lights. "Besides, you own a car like a Ferrari, and you're a target. Someone will try and take it off you, or vandalize it, and you're more likely to get speeding tickets. Driving a foreign sports car is like waving a red rag at the cops. I prefer a quieter life.''

Her eyelids drooped to shield her eyes from the sun as West turned into traffic, but she felt surprisingly alert. The last conversation she'd had with West concerning what kind of life he wanted had ended up with him walking out on the marriage because quiet and settled were the last things he wanted. ''I heard you tell Farrell you'd left the SAS.''

''I resigned a month ago.''

Tyler tensed, her mind abruptly ice-clear. ''Why?''

''I'd been in for twelve years. Most guys don't stay for more than nine or ten. I'd had enough—I needed out.''

His terse statement that he needed out was startling. Even though common sense told her that no one could live at the intense level demanded by special forces for too many years, somehow, the normal rules hadn't seemed to apply to West. Maybe because it had been such an issue between them, she'd always assumed he'd stay in forever.

West pulled into the car park of a mall which included a medical center and strolled into the sprawling, multi-level complex. When he emerged, he had a paper bag with a chemist's logo on it, and a bottle of water.

He slid into the driver's seat, handed her the water

and the bag. "Voltaren for the inflammation. Codeine for the pain."

She took the pills and sipped the bottled water as he drove. Minutes later, as they turned into the underground entrance to the apartment building, her stomach tensed, and the question that had been driving her quietly crazy ever since she'd practically walked into him in the garage just days ago surfaced.

He slotted the car into his space, placed his sunglasses on the dash, and killed the engine. The abrupt silence was unnerving.

She removed her own sunglasses and slipped them into her handbag, relieved that the faint pressure they'd exerted on her head was gone. "What are you doing here, West?"

"Bringing you home."

"That wasn't what I meant. What are you doing in my building?"

He unclipped his belt. As he turned toward her, Tyler's heart pounded harder than it had done when she was attacked last night. This close she could smell the warm, male scent of his skin, the fresh, faintly resinous scent of his hair, and see a tiny feather inscribed on the stud in his ear. On most men that earring would have looked feminine; on West it just looked exotic.

In the dim lighting of the garage his face was shadowed, his gaze, without the barrier of dark glasses, cool and calm and direct.

"I'm here because I want another chance with you."

Chapter 6

For a moment Tyler couldn't take in what West had said, then the bluntness of the statement hit.

His expression was so impassive that for a moment she wondered if she'd gone a little haywire and imagined he'd said he wanted another chance with her. West wanting to be involved with her on any level other than the tying up of their legal loose ends just didn't make any kind of sense. Then his gaze connected with hers again.

Her heart was still pounding, and her chest felt constricted as if there wasn't enough room for the oxygen she needed. ''What if I'm not interested?''

''Then I'll leave you alone.''

Only, despite everything that was wrong with her and West as a couple, she *was* interested—that was the problem—and she was pretty sure he knew it.

She stared at the concrete wall in front of the car. The number of West's apartment was stenciled on the wall, denoting his space. He had moved in on the third floor, and occupied the apartment two floors directly above hers. She knew because she'd already been up there to check. "It's been *five* years. Why didn't you just ring?"

"You would have hung up."

There was nothing to argue about there. Chances were she would have slammed the phone down in honor of all the times she'd wanted him to ring and he hadn't.

The silence began to unnerve her. She shifted her gaze to the clean line of his jaw. He turned, and she found herself looking him directly in the eye. It was a mistake. West's eyes had always been mesmerizing. Sometimes the tawny gold had been soft, molten; whenever he'd left for a mission they'd been flat, cold and so distant it was as if he'd already left. Now, his gaze was curiously still, utterly focused on her. He wasn't pushing for answers or any kind of a commitment, he was simply stating his intent.

She'd imagined all sorts of scenarios for winding up their relationship—for closure—this wasn't one of them.

Against all odds, against her will, an aching hunger flared to life. If he'd looked at her this way five years ago she would have been in heaven.

Five years.

They'd been hard years, damn him. It had taken

her at least two years to get over him, the other three to feel whole. If she wasn't so sore, she would slug him.

Something fierce and bright flared in his eyes.

"If there was another way to go about this, I would have found it."

Abruptly, he pulled the key from the lock and climbed out of the car. The gesture made him suddenly vulnerable, and the crack in his composure rocked her.

West was—had been—a special forces soldier, a member of one of the most elite fighting units in the world. She knew he was also a businessman, in partnership with the Lombards, cutting the same swathe through boardrooms as he had in the arena of covert operations. Above all, he was a loner. Even when she'd thought he'd been in love with her, he'd been controlled, complete within himself.

She'd expected to feel a range of emotions when she finally confronted West: anger, regret, a big dose of indifference—relief that their long-drawn-out relationship was finally over.

Panic that the relationship might possibly continue wasn't on that list.

The last time she'd run away from anything, she'd been a child escaping an abusive father, but she felt like running now.

Eight years ago, they'd both been young and the attraction that had flared between them had burned out of control from the beginning. They'd married quickly, and the marriage had fallen apart just as fast. West had been gone more often than not, and she'd never known where he was, when he'd be back or even *if* he'd be back. He'd been like a big hunting cat: remote and a little scary. His occupation as a sniper-team commander had defined him. He'd been almost frighteningly controlled and observant and meticulous about detail—but one detail had escaped him: their marriage.

Even when they'd made love she'd had no sense of holding him beyond the tangible evidence of his physical presence at that moment—and their marriage certificate. When he was called away on an assignment, each time he'd shut her out as easily as he'd closed the door behind him when he left.

She unclipped her seat belt, found the strap of her bag, hooked it over her shoulder and girded herself for the ordeal of getting herself out of the car. Apparently, according to her body, it was an intricate process involving the use of every muscle and nerve she owned.

She pushed her door open, but before she could make a move, West was there, his hand extended.

Without thinking she accepted his grip. His hand was warm, his hold firm, and she was instantly reminded of the way he'd steadied her last night; the sheer, shuddering relief when he'd magically appeared at the exact moment that she'd needed help.

She'd tried to make light of the attack to Richard and Harrison by labeling it a mugging, not wanting to alarm them any further when they already had so much to worry about, but the swiftness and brutality of the attack had, quite frankly, terrified her.

There had been a coldness—a level of calculation—that took it beyond a simple mugging, although maybe that was simply the shock talking. Maybe every mugging victim felt that the attack was personal. But whether she had been a specific target or a random one, she still felt cold inside at the possibilities if West hadn't intervened.

He'd rescued her twice within the space of a few hours. Relationship issues aside, as a guardian angel his timing was perfect.

Tyler unlocked her door and stepped into her apartment. West followed close behind. The air felt overly warm, and the apartment itself smelled slightly stuffy because it had been closed up for almost two days.

There was mail on her kitchen counter, and she saw with relief that her kitten's bowl was full of cat biscuits and that there was a clean dish of water. Harrison must have rung Maia, a friend of Tyler's who lived in one of the other ground-floor apartments, and got her to feed Tiger and collect the mail.

West carried her overnight bag into the lounge, then walked through to the kitchen, making the cosy room seem suddenly tiny. "Sit down and I'll get you a drink. You're out on your feet."

Tyler debated refusing, but she was in no condition to refuse help, especially when lately she had done nothing but accept help from West.

Her mind still skittered past the mystifying fact that after five years he wanted her at all—that he was committed to the point that he had actually moved into her building. It had all happened too quickly, but West's agenda, difficult to accept as it was, didn't frighten her. He might want her back, but wild as he'd been when she first met him, as lethal as she knew he must have been as a special forces soldier, she knew that she was intrinsically safe with him. He would never push the issue.

She sank into an armchair in the lounge, listening to West in the kitchen, feeling boneless and slightly dozy. The codeine and the Voltaren she'd taken were finally kicking in, so that all she wanted to do was sink farther and farther into the chair.

West brought her a cup of tea, which she sipped slowly while he opened the doors to her terrace and let fresh air in. He also must have opened the kitchen windows, because a delicious breeze flowed through the room. She watched through half-closed lids as he walked out onto the terrace, which was bathed in sunlight, the absence of shadows indicating that the day had slipped by, and it must be close to lunchtime. When he strode back inside, he paused beside a selection of bags that sat to one side of the room.

She yawned and set the tea down. "I have an addiction. It's called shopping. Last week I was on a hair trigger."

''What did you buy?''

She looked at the bright assortment of bags. They'd been gathering dust for a week. Normally she loved sorting through her purchases, but in this case she'd gone late-night shopping the evening before the jade had been stolen. When she'd gotten home she'd simply dumped the packages, meaning to deal with them when she got in from work the next evening, but the next day they'd discovered the jade was missing and all hell had broken loose. Since then, she'd only been back to the apartment to sleep and had barely noticed the bags, let alone paid them any attention. She was barely able to remember what she'd bought.

He pulled out a box, lifted the lid.

She had bought shoes. Lots of them.

She vaguely remembered that the reason she'd gone shopping was that the summer sales were on. It had only been last week, but it felt like a lifetime ago.

His mouth kicked up at one corner. ''What happened? You had a blackout experience, found yourself out on the street with the bags—your card seriously damaged? Or did the aliens abduct you?''

The hint of amusement in his voice, his gaze, riveted her, and for a moment she wondered if she was imagining this conversation. ''The aliens?''

''The ones that make you go shopping.''

A smile tugged at her mouth, and she gingerly touched her fingers to her lips to stop her smile from getting too wide. Smiling *hurt.* ''You know about shopping.''

He went down on his haunches next to the bags, began extracting boxes and opening them. ''I like to shop.''

Next to killing people.

She watched, dazed, as he dangled a strappy, candy-pink pair of high-heeled shoes from one lean brown finger. They had something in common.

How come she hadn't remembered that? A man who not only liked to shop but who understood the blackout syndrome.

If the news got out he'd be mobbed.

West pulled out a pair of boxing gloves. ''You *box?*''

He met Tyler's gaze. In the afternoon sunlight her eyes were a cool, clear green. She looked pale, tousled, but very calm.

An inner shift, fierce and possessive, made his spine tighten and his belly clench. He'd always loved her face, loved the delicate slant to her cheekbones, the strength in her jaw, but now he felt as if he were seeing her for the first time. He knew the pressures and strains that had hammered and reshaped him over the last five years. Covert work was an uneasy crucible—if the bad guys didn't get you, the stress did—but he had no idea what had shaped Tyler.

The change was subtle, but powerful. He'd missed it before, because ever since he'd moved into the building, Tyler had avoided looking directly at him.

She'd avoided him, period. And over the last few hours she'd been too hurt and too woozy to do anything more than survive the hospital process and the police interviews.

He'd glimpsed the new inner toughness when she'd come to on the car-park floor after being hit last night. Now he could see it in her steady gaze, feel it in the calm strength that radiated from her. Tyler was female, but he was suddenly aware that that was only a detail. Gender aside, she was as fierce and extreme as any warrior.

She picked up her cup of tea and cradled it between both hands. "I took up boxing a couple of years ago after a friend got attacked outside a nightclub. Billie can walk now, but she spent months in traction and even longer in rehab. At the time, the punch bag was therapeutic."

West set the gloves down and rose to his feet; the reason she'd chosen boxing over more fashionable gym sports was clear. It was physical and immediate, a pure channel for aggression.

He knew guys who did martial arts and guys who boxed. Without exception he would always want the boxer at his back in a fight because he knew the guy would have an edge over the purist martial arts expert. He would have the killer instinct. In Special Forces they were taught to integrate martial arts with boxing and street fighting. The rule was that any one technique wasn't the key; you just used what you had to to get the job done. If you could complete the mission without making any noise or harming anyone, so much the better, but if a bad guy fronted up doing judo and you had a gun, you pulled the gun and shot him.

His gaze shifted to her scraped knuckles. "No wonder you broke the guy's jaw."

She knew how to move, how to swing to give her punch maximum power. Respect for the way Tyler had defended herself settled in his stomach. The reason she'd bruised her hand so badly was because she'd punched as if she was gloved.

He wondered which A&E the hurt guy had ended up in. Cornell would follow it up, but West would be right on his tail. "Do many people know you box?"

"Harrison and Richard. I don't know that anyone else does. It's not something that comes up in conversations. Why?"

West shrugged. "In an investigation, sometimes the most unlikely piece of information can help eliminate suspects and solve the crime. Those guys who attacked you last night got taken by surprise."

"Maybe. Or maybe they discounted the fact that I could box. In any case, it still leaves a cast of thousands who could have mugged me. And the mugging investigation is turning out to be about as conclusive as the jade one."

"Cornell's good, so is Farrell. Between the two of them they'll slice and dice the information until there's nothing left to learn, then they'll start making patterns. If anyone can find the thief, they can.''

There was a brief silence. ''You don't believe I'm the thief?''

West caught the hurt in the question, and his chest tightened. He'd known she was having a bad time. He also knew just what it was like to stand accused by people who were secure in their belief that even if he hadn't done the crime, he should do the time. ''Cornell doesn't either. He's a good judge of character.''

She went very still, her face pale, and he swore beneath his breath. Cornell was good—there was no getting past it—but he was also ruthless. He'd left Tyler dangling because he was more likely to get details that she might otherwise overlook, or forget, if she was secure in the knowledge that Cornell believed her to be innocent.

Tyler's doorbell chimed, the small sound breaking the tension.

West straightened. ''Stay there,'' he said grimly. ''I'll get it.''

Tyler heard the low register of West's voice, then a lighter female voice.

Maia breezed cheerfully into the lounge, rolling her eyes at West—who had followed on behind her—and clutching at her heart. She was dressed in workout gear, her holdall slung over her shoulder, boxing gloves just visible tucked in next to a towel.

Maia was olive-skinned, gorgeous and happily single. She worked long hours as a chef at a Newmarket café and kept cats instead of men. She said that, shedding fur aside, cats were clean and cuddly and low maintenance, as opposed to her ex. She'd made the naive mistake of marrying without a prenuptial agreement, and it had cost her her business. Two years AD, which stood for two years After Darren, she was finally approaching the point where she could invest in her own café again.

She bent and hugged Tyler, exclaimed over the mugging and her stitches, and deposited another bundle of mail and a paper on the coffee table beside Tyler's chair.

She examined Tyler's bruised knuckles. "Ouch!" You're supposed to work out, girl, not get worked over."

Maia jerked her head in the direction of the kitchen, where West was drinking a glass of water at the counter, and whispered, "Who's *that?*"

"Remember when we had that discussion about marriage?"

She grinned. "Been there, done that. Can't remember most of it. Thank God."

"Well, that's my ex."

Maia darted another look at West. She fanned herself. "Oh—my—God. No wonder you don't date."

She stayed for a few more minutes, catching Tyler up to date on the latest goings-on in the building. How the Morgans, a middle-aged couple in 4A who had given up hope of ever having a child, were now expecting a baby, and how Mirna in 5D had decided at age sixty that she'd somehow missed out on the joy of a midlife crisis, and had promptly found herself a boyfriend who was ten years younger, and who drove a 'Vette.

Maia glanced at her watch and halted in mid-flow, exclaiming that she was going to be late. She gave Tyler a final hug, then left for her gym appointment with a last eye-rolling glance at West.

Tyler continued to sit in the chair. She felt utterly relaxed, bordering on floaty. She reached for her tea, and misjudged, her fingers brushing the pile of mail and sending it cascading onto the floor. The paper flopped half off the coffee table. Tyler caught it before it could slide onto the floor, glanced at the front page, and went cold inside.

The small black-and-white was grainy, but there was no mistaking Sonny Mullane, her natural father. He was thinner, older, his hair sparser—gray instead of chestnut-brown—but still swept back from his forehead in a widow's peak. His nose looked larger and coarser, a consequence of the booze, but his dark eyes were just as sharp.

She pulled the paper onto her lap. The article was situated at the bottom of the page, and was billed as a candid interview about his life with her. According to Sonny the welfare state had let them down, and they'd had to steal or starve. Now Tyler was living in the lap of luxury and poor old Sonny was a sickness beneficiary struggling to make ends meet.

Tyler's jaw tightened. Odds were that he was using false identities and pulling in more than one welfare benefit. And with Sonny, food had always been secondary to the bottle; she was the only one who had ever gone hungry. Everything they'd owned had been converted into cheap sherry, until finally they'd been out on the streets, and Sonny had decided that he had one more commodity to sell—his eight-year-old daughter. Even at that young age, she'd known what would happen to her if she'd stayed with Sonny, and she'd frozen inside; she'd seen the prostitutes working in cars and back alleys.

For as long as she could remember, she'd taken beating after beating from Sonny, but had clung to him, because in a hostile world, he was her only living relative. She'd spent time in hospital and in foster homes, but Sonny had always managed to get her back. This time she'd made sure he couldn't do that. When he'd come to get her, he'd been arrested, and on her testimony, he'd served a prison term. Shortly after that, Tyler had gone to live with the Laine family.

She wondered how much the newspapers had paid him for the story. She stared at the bold headline, and her stomach knotted.

Apparently, he'd taught her to steal.

Chapter 7

West skimmed the article, his gaze cold. ''How did they manage to track down your old man?''

''Knowing Sonny, he would have knocked on their door.'' She rose to her feet, steadying herself against the arm of the chair. In the brief time that she had been sitting, all of her sore muscles had tightened, so that moving at all was painful. ''If you don't mind, I'm going to lie down.''

He folded the paper. ''I'm not leaving.''

''I'm perfectly okay now, I don't need—''

His gaze glittered over her. ''You're head-injured. Last night you were attacked in the car park. The press is hounding you, you've been followed, and someone's been phoning you—''

''You heard.''

"Yeah, I caught that bit, and I'm glad I did. But even if I hadn't, I still wouldn't leave you on your own right now. Call it gut instinct, call it what you like, but I'm not leaving until I know you're safe. I've done a quick check of some of your window and door locks. They're adequate, but for a ground-floor apartment, they're not foolproof."

Tyler's stomach tightened at West's certainty that she needed protection. His perceptions had always been uncannily sharp, and sometimes he had just known things—like who was phoning, or who was at the door. Once, he'd packed his gear to go away when he hadn't been due to go for several days. He'd gotten the call to leave in the middle of the night, and had been gone within minutes.

Her jaw squared. Uneasy or not, she still didn't want him in her apartment overnight. "I can make you leave."

West met her gaze flatly. "You and whose army? Call the cops if you like, but I'm staying the rest of the day—and the night. I'll sleep on the couch."

Tyler closed the door of her room behind her and sagged against it. The thought that her own apartment wasn't secure, that *she* wasn't safe, shouldn't have shocked her. Richard had tried to make the same point earlier, but she'd cut him off, choosing instead to cling to the illusion of safety that her home represented.

Like it or not, she was in trouble.

Just how much trouble, she didn't know, but the list of things that had gone wrong for her lately was growing at a frightening pace, just when she'd finally reached a point in her life when everything should have been perfect.

In her own mind she'd categorized all the events that had happened to her as separate misfortunes. Her suspicion that she had been followed and the coincidence of the phone calls happening at the same time had been eerie, but none of the instances had tied into any solid evidence that she *was* being stalked, certainly not enough to warrant a complaint to the police.

The idea that someone could actually be stalking her was abruptly unreal, as unreal as her father stepping out of the past to take one more shot at selling his daughter.

The grainy photo of her father rose up in her mind, making her stomach clench—an old reaction to an old fear. As attacks went, the media was the least of her problems, but the story had dug deep into her personal life, once more pushing home just how vulnerable and exposed she was to the press. The article had consisted of malicious gossip, outright lies and a small foundation of truth, but regardless of the content, it had done its damage.

She had become a liability to Laine's.

She had already decided that if the mystery of the jade theft wasn't solved and her credibility restored, she would resign.

Harrison would argue. He was a gentleman to his bones and had encouraged her every step of the way with her studies and her career. When she'd gained her doctorate, he'd been fiercely proud of her. But losing the few years she'd dedicated to her career didn't come close to what was at stake for her family's business.

Laine's dealt in artifacts and antiquities, but diamonds were where the real money was made. The business arena of the diamond trade was small, hugely wealthy, and utterly merciless. Any hint that Harrison Laine had lost his grip to the extent that he was continuing to employ a family member who was suspected of theft, and his lines of supply would dry up.

No matter how determined he was to protect her, she wouldn't allow him to compromise his reputation and his business for the sake of her career.

The steps she would have to take to cut ties to the business and the career she loved sent a cold chill through Tyler. Once she resigned, her career was effectively over. She wouldn't work with artifacts or jade again.

It was also possible that she would have to go away. And once she left, she would have to stay away.

She'd thought the process through, and each time the solution was the same. For her strategy to be effective, she would not only have to leave her career, she would have to be seen to separate herself from her family.

She could feel the grief lurking just below some invisible barrier in her consciousness, a sharp little ache waiting to overwhelm her, but her mind had reached saturation point and she was suddenly incapable of thinking, incapable of feeling.

Her eyes drooped, closed, and refused to open. Her body felt heavy and curiously disconnected, the door a cool, solid anchor at her back. She took a deep breath, she pushed away from the door and willed herself to take the few steps needed to reach the bed, frightened that if she didn't move now, she'd go to sleep while she was on her feet, then fall and knock her head again. She took two steps toward the bed, then a third. The front of her knees connected with the edge of the queen-sized bed, and she half toppled, half crawled onto it, and curled on her side, too exhausted to get undressed or pull anything over herself. She inched her shoes off, heard them plop on the floor. All of the tension gradually seeped from her limbs. She felt boneless, heavy, her mind blank as she finally gave in to the pull of sleep and slid down into darkness.

West did a quick tour of Tyler's apartment. Aside from the fact that it was situated on the ground floor, it was an exact duplicate of his own; three bedrooms, a study, a spacious lounge and a small kitchen, with a separate dining area. But that was where the similarity ended. His place was classy, nice—it could have been pulled from the pages of a designer magazine—but it was essentially empty of character, and he hadn't bothered to inject any. He already owned a house just a few minutes' drive away, and he didn't envisage keeping the apartment any longer than it took to get Tyler back.

Tyler's apartment was crammed with comfortable furniture, books, potted plants and bright, quirky prints. She had lived here for the past three years and it showed.

A whirring sound behind him made him turn. A small cat was sitting just inside the cat flap—a dainty little multi-colored ball of fluff with crazy markings on its face and calm, curious eyes. A second cat sat beside it—this one larger and stripey.

West went down on his haunches and waited until the cats approached. After a few seconds, they sniffed at his fingers and nuzzled into his palm, tails swishing. The fluffy one was female, the stripey, a male.

Both cats walked pointedly toward the kitchen. West followed and found them grouped around a set of bowls with Tiger emblazoned on the sides.

"Tiger One and Tiger Two, huh?"

His mouth twitched. He'd never had a pet—he had never been at home long enough to have one—but he liked animals, and for some odd reason they seemed to like him. "So, what do you eat when you're not scaring up mice?"

There were already biscuits and water there, so he found milk in the refrigerator and filled a bowl, then examined the pantry and found a can of designer cat food and emptied it into a second bowl. The tuna was delicately flaked and looked good enough to eat. A few months ago, on extended patrol, he would have killed for some of this stuff. Standard army issue rations came in cans, tubes, some of it was freeze-dried and shrink-wrapped in plastic and foil. You had to be hungry to eat most of it, and it wasn't packaged to attract, just to travel.

The cats tucked in, ate the tuna, then delicately licked at the milk. When they were finished, they trotted past him, crawled out of the cat flap and disappeared.

West made some calls. He didn't like it that the apartment complex, which was supposedly secure, had been so open to attack. In theory no one but a resident should have been able to gain access to the underground garage, but there was nothing too sinister about one of the remote-control devices that activated the gates to the apartment complex—and the PIN that went with it—being stolen. But someone had not only gained access to the complex, they had also located the fuse box in the service area of the building and knocked out the lighting for the entire garage.

This morning, before he'd gone to the hospital, West had talked to the maintenance service that looked after the building. There was an alarm system on the electrics, so that if anything blew, the specific area that had failed flashed up on their screens and they could respond instantly. Last night the first indication they'd had that something was wrong was when a resident had phoned in complaining that the garage was blacked out. That meant that the men who had attacked Tyler had also gone to the trouble of researching the building's maintenance system and had found out how to disable the alarm.

The only working lights in the area had been those attached to the elevators, but it made sense to leave those alone. If they'd knocked out the elevator lights, they would have run the risk that any resident who used the elevator would have been alerted to the power failure and would have called maintenance in, which would have interfered with the crime.

The planning and premeditation behind the mugging seemed out of all proportion to what had actually happened. They had left Tyler's handbag alone and had targeted her briefcase. That wasn't so unusual in itself if the thieves were specifically after a laptop and were stealing to order, but this crime didn't bear any of the hallmarks of that kind of organized theft. What they'd gained was minimal compared to the effort they'd expended, and he would have expected them to have snatched the purse when the opportunity presented itself.

When West had spent time on the streets, he'd known gangs who stole to order. They were organized, methodical and ruthlessly practical—they kept the risk factor as low as possible, and they didn't expend one bit of energy they didn't have to. The name of the game was the same as in any business—profit.

Tyler had lost her computer, but, big deal, that kind of theft happened every day, and in this case the insurance money would replace the computer. He knew from the statement that she'd given to the police that she had also backed up all her work on disk, so the physical harm that had been done to her aside, other than the inconvenience of making the insurance claim and buying another briefcase and laptop, Tyler hadn't lost a thing.

When he'd bought his apartment, the security had seemed adequate, although not top-notch, but West hadn't cared about the security specs, or about any aspect of the complex other than it was where Tyler lived. Now he was more than interested. Something was badly wrong, and Tyler was at the center of it.

He didn't know if last night's attack had anything to do with the theft of the jade. Maybe the two events were completely unrelated, and the fact that the attack had happened so soon after the theft was a coincidence? But West didn't like coincidences—especially not when they involved Tyler.

Tyler woke late in the afternoon. She sat up slowly. Her head still throbbed, and she was still stiff and sore, but she felt better than she had this morning. Gingerly, she flexed the fingers of her right hand. The swelling had gone down, and the grazes on her knuckles had begun to heal over, but the bruising was now spectacular.

A yawn rolled through her. Gingerly, she swung her feet to the floor, and pushed hair back from her face.

Rich sunlight poured in through the bifold doors which opened onto a leafy terrace, filling the room with dappled golden light. She checked the bedside clock and saw that it was nearly six o'clock, which explained why she was so thirsty and her stomach felt so hollow. She'd slept for approximately six hours. Beside the clock, there was a sandwich on a plate, covered in plastic wrap, a glass of water and some pills.

The bedside phone rang, but before she could pick it up, the ringing stopped, and she heard the low rumble of West's voice as he answered the call in the lounge.

She blinked, adjusting all over again to the fact that West had not only brought her home, but he was still in her apartment and intending to stay the night.

She nibbled at the sandwich, took more painkillers and Voltaren, and drank the water. After using her en suite bathroom, she crawled back into bed and laid her head carefully on the pillow. The phone rang again, minutes later a door opened and closed, and she heard the clink of crockery.

Her eyelids drifted closed. It seemed that after

days without being able to sleep, now all her body wanted to do was rest.

Another yawn worked its way up from deep in her belly, leaving her feeling limp and exhausted, and she let sleep pull her under again.

A man dressed in black pants, a black crew neck sweatshirt and black sneakers exited his car. He extracted a small matte-black backpack from the passenger seat, closed the door, then strolled away, half turning to lock the vehicle. There was no cheerful beeping, no flash of car lights, just the gentle thunk of the lock engaging.

Seconds later, he approached an imposing plastered wall which surrounded an expensive apartment complex. He took a pair of thin black leather gloves from his pocket, pulled them on, shrugged into the backpack, then gripped the gnarled limb of a large pohutukawa tree and levered himself up and over the wall with fluid ease.

During the day, the pohutukawa was a spectacular sight, its limbs spreading far enough to shade several metres of pavement and part of the road. The tree was large enough and old enough that it would have a protection order on it. No doubt the speculators who had built the apartment block had seen the tree as an asset to the value of the property—which it was—but it completely negated the security of the wall.

He turned north, walking in the direction of a dark

clump of ornamental shrubs that butted up against the wall. When he was within the thick shelter of the shrubs, he extracted a penlight torch from his pocket and squatted down beside a gray metal telecommunications box—the external siting of which was another fault of these older apartment blocks.

He grinned coldly. The hell he would ever invest in such a sloppy operation.

Setting the torch down, he eased out of the backpack, extracted his laptop and set it down on the dirt. The door of the box hung a little ajar, which meant that no one had been to check it since he'd jimmied the lock open a week ago. Satisfied that the security personnel who serviced the apartment block were still unaware that the box had been tampered with, he propped the torch so that it would shine into the interior of the box, then pulled the door open, removed the internal plastic housing, and examined the thick, multi-colored snake of coded wires.

He separated the strands that he'd previously selected and stripped, and slotted the wires into a standard plug. Seconds later he plugged his laptop in and booted the computer. The screen lit up, and with a few keystrokes, he had the building's security system on line. He keyed in a password and waited for verification. It was possible that the password had changed from the last time he'd used it, in which case he would resort to a password-breaking program—but that necessity wasn't likely. He'd already researched the security firm that had done this installation, and had visited two of their sites, posing as a repairman. In all instances the same password had been used. They might be in the business of security, but like a lot of people, when it came to passwords and PINs, they clung to stupidity, using simple-to-crack passwords for the same dumb reason: they didn't want to forget the password themselves.

Seconds later, the security firm's logo and menu appeared. He tapped a key, and the specs for the building flashed onto the screen. Anticipation rolled in his stomach.

He was in.

Chapter 8

Tyler woke, abruptly alert—her head clear. She lay still and silent. Something had woken her. A sound.

She waited for the sound to come again and became aware that her room was completely dark, the absence of light so profound that for a moment disorientation gripped her, and she lost her bearings completely.

A chill tightened her spine. She couldn't remember pulling the drapes, so West must have done that, and the fact that she was now covered with a quilt bore out the fact that he'd come into her room to check on her, but there should still be some light.

Usually the streetlamps and the external security lighting threw a faint glow into all of the rooms. The glow was especially visible around the edges of the drapes, but now the blackness was so complete, she couldn't make out where the wall finished and the drapes began.

The only explanation was that the power must have been cut, but she couldn't think of any logical reason for that to happen. There was no wild weather to interfere with utility services, and she hadn't been notified of any planned power outages. Any cuts would compromise the building's security system, so usually residents were notified well in advance.

She turned her head just enough on the pillow that she could see her digital clock. The faint luminosity of the numbers told her that it was one-thirty in the morning, and that the power *was* on. The fact that the clock wasn't flashing told her the power hadn't been interfered with, which meant that only the power to the streetlights and the security lighting was off.

A faint clunk came from the direction of her dresser—as if someone had placed an item down on the polished surface.

Adrenaline flooded her system. Tyler's heart slammed hard in her chest, and for a frozen moment she couldn't breathe, couldn't think. After the mugging last night, she wouldn't have thought anything else could go wrong, but something had.

Someone was in the room with her.

West came out of sleep fast.

He didn't know what had woken him, and he

didn't question why he was awake, he just knew that something was wrong.

The lack of any discernible light registered, and his heart slammed in his chest, the jolt of adrenaline flooding his system little more than a convenient tool that took him from normal to battle-ready in a heartbeat.

Either the power was out, or they had company.

A quick glance at the television told him that, despite the pitch blackness, the power to the apartment hadn't been interfered with because the small standby light was still glowing.

One of the cats was asleep on his chest. Gently, he moved the furry weight to one side, shoved free of the blanket he'd pulled over his legs, and rolled to his feet. He stood for a moment, adjusting to the darkness and soaking in the unfamiliar scents of the room, the distant, muted sounds of the city. He was still dressed in jeans, and he didn't bother pulling on his T-shirt as he navigated the coffee table and an armchair, his bare feet soundless on the carpeted floor.

He didn't have a weapon, but in the pitch dark, a weapon was a secondary consideration. He knew the layout of the apartment; his main concern was the exact placement of furniture in each room because he hadn't had time to familiarize himself completely.

When he reached Tyler's door, he paused, listening. Maybe he was overreacting, but he didn't think so. The two men who had assaulted Tyler last night had interfered with the power. For it to happen a second time was too much of a coincidence for West to accept.

Gently, he eased the door open, his mind coldly sliding through his options as he stepped into the room. In that instant he could feel the presence, as palpably as if he'd walked into a wall. The base of his neck tightened on a cold tingle as he tried to orient himself by forming a mental picture of the room, at the same time letting his mind go loose as he tried to locate the exact position of the intruder.

His attention centered on a stirring of movement. A split second later, light flared, burning into his retinas. Tyler yelled out his name, and sound exploded against the far wall.

West had an instant freeze-frame of the curtain swinging, as if someone had just gone through the bifold door, and Tyler standing on the far side of her bed, digital clock in her hand, ready to launch a second missile. As he sprang across the room, shoved the curtain aside and went through the open door, he realized that the explosion of sound had been a glass smashing against the far wall.

He paused to hear in what direction the intruder had gone, then lost precious seconds, navigating pots and shrubs before hitting the lawn at a flat run. He knew the general layout of the main gardens around the apartment complex, but he hadn't had time to familiarize himself with any of it yet. Until now, he hadn't seen the need—he'd been focused on Tyler—and now he cursed his lack of knowledge.

He could hear the intruder ahead of him, but he couldn't see him, partly because the light had destroyed his night vision, but also because the bad guy was dressed all in black. There was no pale gleam of flesh to give away his position, which meant he must also be wearing black gloves and a black stocking or a balaclava.

The gloves marked him out as a professional. Most amateurs would cover their faces because they didn't want to be identified, but they generally forgot about their hands, and whether it was day or night, skin reflected light—and in the dark, pale skin glowed.

Apart from the light flooding from Tyler's room, it was very dark, which was odd for the city. There was no street lighting—he must have knocked that out—and if there was a moon it was hidden behind a thick blanket of cloud.

Last night he'd had the cover of the storm to act; tonight, he'd created the conditions he needed to commit the crime.

West didn't question that the perpetrator was the same. Two nights in a row the power had been interfered with and Tyler had been attacked. He didn't know what the motive was, yet. All he knew was that it was the same guy.

Movement flickered up higher than he expected.

West cursed, and circumnavigated the ghostly outline of a clump of palms. He was going over the wall.

Seconds later he reached the wall, grabbed the gnarled limb of a tree, pulled himself up onto the broad top and sprang down onto the other side. As his bare feet hit the pavement, he heard the slam of a car door, caught the red flash of taillights. A car accelerated away—already too distant for him to catch the plate.

West stopped, sucked in a deep breath and let it out slowly. He was hardly panting; he was fit, but that didn't change the fact that the bad guy had run rings around him because he knew the territory, and West didn't.

He stared silently down the empty street. That wouldn't happen again.

Tyler walked through the apartment, chills racing down her spine as she switched on every light.

When she'd been mugged in the garage, both men had been little more than black shadows, dehumanized by the balaclavas that had blanked out their faces, but she'd been able to see the threat, and when she'd hit out, she'd been able to hurt them. This time there had been only one man, and she hadn't seen him at all. He'd used the smothering darkness as both concealment and a weapon. The cold terror of those moments in her bedroom were still with her, like a core of ice in her belly.

She walked into the kitchen. The clock on the wall said it was twenty to two. Only ten minutes had passed since she'd woken to find someone in her room, touching her things. Considering everything that had happened in those minutes, the brief span of time seemed ludicrously short.

Abruptly, she relived the moment when West had, once again, materialized out of the darkness in the exact instant she'd needed him. His gaze had touched on hers, both fierce and remote, then he'd flowed across the room, flung the curtain aside and disappeared into the night.

She stared through the window, and another spasm of chills attacked her spine.

She'd lived in this city all her life. She'd experienced the seamier side as a child—she knew about bad, and she knew about evil—but the cold, systematic way the perpetrator had tampered with the lighting and broken into her home had stripped away another subtle layer of gray. Tonight, she'd run smack into evil.

Automatically, she filled the electric jug with water and switched it on, then placed the tea canister and two mugs on the bench—using the age-old ritual of making tea to settle her nerves. She didn't know if West still drank tea, but he used to, and she needed to do something while she waited for him to come back.

That he would come back, she didn't doubt.

As Tyler reached for the sugar bowl, her bone-deep, unquestioning confidence in West as a professional soldier—a warrior—dissolved the cold knot of tension in her belly and abruptly balanced the scales.

A primitive satisfaction filled her. As evil as the bad guy was, she wouldn't want to be in his shoes when West got hold of him.

When West walked back across the lawn to Tyler's apartment, all the lights were blazing. Tyler was in the kitchen making a hot drink, her jeans and shirt rumpled, hair tousled around her face.

She handed him a mug. Her gaze raked him from head to toe. "Are you all right?"

The demand was husky and flat, the look completely female—the kind of look women had been giving their husbands and sons since time immemorial. "I didn't get near him. He went over the wall by that big pohutukawa. His car was parked just up the street." West took a sip of the hot drink, awareness sliding through him that Tyler's glance hadn't been all about safety. "I was too late to get the license plate."

She cupped her mug between her hands as if she was chilled, despite the warm temperature, and he caught the fine tremor in her fingers. "He did something to knock the power out." She didn't say, "It's the same guy," but the knowledge was there in her gaze.

His jaw tightened. "Did he touch you?"

"He didn't get the chance."

Some of West's tension dissipated. So, okay, the son of a bitch could live. Just.

He glanced at the microwave clock, which was

showing the correct time. That meant there hadn't been an interruption of the power supply, just selective tampering.

An image of the guy running through the night, little more than a flickering shadow, flashed through his mind, and frustration and temper ate at his control. The slick bastard knew his stuff. He'd prepared his op and carried it out with precision. The only hitch had been that he hadn't factored West into the equation.

"He cut the power to the streetlights for a couple of blocks, and turned the security system off, but this time he'd left the power supply to the complex alone."

That had been smart. If he'd interfered with the power, someone might have noticed and alerted the maintenance crew, or rung the police. "I'm going to put a call through to Cornell. Why don't you pack a few things? We can move to my apartment for what's left of the night. A few minutes from now this place is going to be a zoo."

"I've already phoned Cornell. He's on his way."

To West's surprise, Tyler didn't argue about moving to his apartment. Within minutes she was packed and ready to go, her overnight bag parked in the hallway to one side of the door. As he rinsed his empty mug and placed it in the dishwasher, she walked into the kitchen with the fluffy kitten cuddled in her arms.

He watched as she tipped more biscuits into the cat's dish, and his fury over the break-in aside, a completely male satisfaction that Tyler would be spending the rest of the night in his apartment and, as it happened, in his bed, settled in his stomach. It was a long way from what he wanted, but more than he'd expected so soon.

Tyler was wary of him, and she had every right to be. It was a cold fact that he'd been lousy relationship material. The first time he'd ever laid eyes on her, he'd instantly known he should have walked away, but he hadn't. He'd asked her to dance, and once he'd touched her, he hadn't wanted to stop. The first kiss had been endless; the second one had come close to getting them both arrested; the third, in the back seat of his car, had almost catapulted them into parenthood. They'd barely made it to his flat in one piece. He'd lost clothes: a leather jacket, his T-shirt. She'd lost her handbag and her underwear.

They'd spent the night and all the next day twined in his bed. A week later, when Tyler had finally gone home, West had gone with her and helped her pack her things. A month later they'd gotten married. Two days after the wedding, he'd been airlifted out to Afghanistan.

The memory of how it had been between them rose up inside him, taking his breath. He had never forgotten the piercing intensity, the bone-deep need. It had shaken him, haunted him. But despite that, he *had* pushed the marriage to one side, and it had taken two shots from Renwick's handgun—both meant for him—and a dying woman he'd thought for one crazy moment was Tyler, to make him understand what losing her would mean.

He'd survived the shooting unscathed, but this time he hadn't been left feeling cold and untouched. The moment had been primitive and powerful, and it had changed him in an instant in a way no amount of discussion or education could ever have done—ripping away the armoured shell he'd built around his emotions, leaving him raw and exposed and sharply aware that, while neither he nor Tyler had died, in all the ways that counted, he *had* lost her.

Grimly, he watched Tyler fussing over the kitten and moving around the kitchen, refilling the kettle and setting it to boil, and placing extra mugs on the kitchen counter. She managed the tasks with an automatic ease, despite the stiffness of her right hand—despite the head injury and the scare she'd had tonight. In fact, she was altogether *too* calm and accepting, especially on one particular subject. "You're not arguing about going to my place."

Tyler spooned coffee grounds into her machine and turned it on. She glanced at West, her gaze stark. "He was in my room, touching my things. I don't know if I ever want to sleep in there again. Your apartment is two stories up. Unless this guy has suction cups on his feet and hands, he won't make it up there."

West eyed her sharply. "Did he take anything?"

"Not that I've noticed. He just seemed to be picking things up and putting them down."

''There aren't likely to be any fingerprints. He was wearing gloves. He might have got cocky enough to take his gloves off when he was dealing with the power and security systems, but I doubt it.''

Tyler opened the fridge, extracted a container of milk and bent down to top up the cat's milk bowl. ''There was something else....'' She straightened, the milk container still in one hand. ''He had something metallic on his head. I couldn't see him, but I knew where he was standing, and when he moved the curtain a little light came in and I caught a glimpse of metal.''

Cold settled at West's nape, the sense of what he could only describe as ''wrongness'' about the attacks on Tyler suddenly acute. ''Night-vision gear.'' The guy was really beginning to tick him off.

If it was possible, Tyler got paler. ''He could see me.''

West let out a breath. ''Yeah, he could see you.''

Cornell and his team arrived about the same time the power board guys and the maintenance service did, but neither of the crews could work until the police had finished dusting for prints. While Tyler was giving her statement, West handed out mugs of coffee and tea.

An hour later, Cornell packed his tape recorder and notebook away in his briefcase. His eyes were bloodshot and his jaw was set. He looked as though he was running on coffee and about two hours' sleep a night. ‘‘This guy’s hurting a whole lot of people. If either the maintenance crew or the power board guys get hold of him, they’re likely to stick a pair of wire cutters in his head.’’

West glanced at the men sitting in the lounge, patiently waiting for clearance to do their jobs. The boss of the power board crew, who was daintily balancing one of Tyler’s bone-china mugs on his knee, was about six-four, two hundred and fifty pounds, with a mullet haircut and biker tattoos on both biceps. The lemon-scented tea he was drinking aside, he looked as if he didn’t take any prisoners. ‘‘They’ll have to stand in line.’’

Chapter 9

West's apartment was bare and distinctly masculine, his style minimalist. He showed her into a bedroom with a broad bed covered in a plain cream coverlet—his bed, and his room—she realized, as he walked past her to throw open a set of bifold doors.

It had started to rain—a slow, heavy pattering—and cool, damp air drifted in from the small paved terrace outside, dissipating the heat that had built up during the day.

West opened drawers and collected fresh clothing, then paused at the door. "There's only the one bed. I'll be sleeping on the couch."

As she watched his broad back disappearing down the hallway, she remembered, with a jolt, that West had moved in here for the specific purpose of getting her back. The apartment was so empty because it didn't need to be filled with furniture. He'd brought the bare necessities required to do the job.

The bareness of the apartment, the fact that he'd uprooted himself from the house she knew he'd bought not long after they'd separated, drove home West's commitment to get her back more effectively than anything else could have done.

He'd told her that he wanted her back; now she believed it.

Tyler unpacked a fresh T-shirt and underwear, then quickly showered before closing the terrace doors and slipping into bed, but once in bed, she couldn't relax. She'd taken more codeine, but despite the medication, she was nowhere near sleepy: she was awake and alert, and her brain wouldn't stop.

After tossing and turning for another few minutes, she switched on the bedside lamp and reached for the new paperback she'd brought with her. Ten pages in, and with no idea what the book was about, she gave up on the story, climbed out of bed, parted the drapes and stared outside. It was still raining, a slow, soothing drumming. She noticed the street-lighting had been restored, but at four in the morning, the roads were empty, the city quiet. She could hear low music playing out in the lounge, the faint clatter of domestic noises, signaling that West was still up; the opening and closing of a cupboard door, a sharp clatter, as if something had dropped on the floor, followed by a plaintive meow.

Tyler went still. West must have gone back to her apartment and collected Tiger. Or, more probably, since Tiger had most probably been outside hunting moths, he'd had to search the grounds for her. Pulling on her jeans and a cotton sweater, she walked out into the lounge, then through into the kitchen.

Her stomach did an odd little flip as she watched him shaking cat biscuits into one of Tiger's bowls. Even though it was unlikely that any intruder would bother a cat, she hadn't liked to think that Tiger could be out there in the dark after what had happened.

"Thanks." She bent down and stroked the fluffy little bundle. Tiger stopped eating long enough to swish her tail and whirr happily.

She noticed he'd even made a litter tray out of a cardboard box and ripped-up newspaper.

A second cat, this one a skinny tabby poked its head out of the laundry, which opened off the kitchen, gave her a blank stare, then ambled over beside Tiger and began chewing on biscuits.

West straightened and set the box of cat biscuits down on the kitchen counter. "I checked your pantry earlier, and you're out of cat food, but they both seemed to be happy with sardines."

Tyler gave him a blank look. "I don't own *two* cats, just Tiger, and I know of only two ground-floor residents who have cats. Old Mr. Rayburn has a big ginger tom called Jaffa, and Maia has two Siamese. This one must be a stray."

West leaned against the counter and folded his arms over his chest. ''Looks like I've got myself a cat then.''

She suppressed a shiver. ''And I need to get a dog. A big dog.'' In all the years she'd lived in the city, she'd never before felt so vulnerable or so powerless. The intruder had broken into the supposedly secure haven of her bedroom while she'd been sunk deep in sleep. Even though she had been fully dressed, and knew how to defend herself, in those first few seconds after waking, she'd felt naked and defenseless. In the dark he had been male and invisible; all the power had been in his hands.

West's gaze caught hers. ''Don't think about it. He didn't touch you, and he won't get near you again.''

''He's gotten to me twice—''

''If he's smart enough to play around with the electrics and the security system, then he's got to know the police are keeping tabs on this place now. He'd have to be certifiable to risk breaking in again.''

''But what if he is certifiable?'' she said quietly. ''What if—''

''Don't.'' His gaze hooked into hers. He said something low beneath his breath, and covered the short gap between them. His hands settled on her arms, his palms burning through the cotton weave of her sweater. ''He broke in because he thought you were vulnerable and alone, and instead he found out that you're protected. In all likelihood he won't be back.''

''In all *likelihood—*''

''Forget I said that.'' His deep voice was exasperated, the first chip in his control she'd yet seen. ''I can't predict what this guy is going to do next, but if he's got any brains he won't come back, because if he does, he'll get caught.''

His hands cupped her neck, his thumbs stroked over her jaw, sending a delicate shiver through her. ''You're shaky—you're probably in shock. Just...be still.''

One big hand settled at her nape, propelling her closer still, until her cheek was resting against his shoulder.

She let out a breath, and let herself relax against him. Her arms wrapped around his waist, and a sharp awareness of how large and solidly muscled he was flooded her. Last night, when she'd been mugged, she'd clung to West, and he'd held on to her, but she'd been too sick to register much; now the heat and tension radiating from him was faintly shocking.

It had been five years since she'd been this physically close to anyone. Now she felt as though she'd buried her head—and her sexuality—in the sand. She'd forgotten how it had been with West—just what he could do to her without trying.

His breath wafted across her temple. The weight of West's hand cupping her nape hadn't changed, but now it sent trails of fire shivering through her, and she felt the intangible moment when comfort faded and a purely physical awareness took over.

He dipped his head. His forehead touched hers.

She lifted her hands to his face, cupped the lean, tanned planes of jaw and cheekbones, looked into his eyes and felt her backbone dissolve and her knees turn to jelly. ‘‘You know, this was something I was never going to do again.’’

‘‘Your choice, not mine.’’

She didn’t try to rehash it. They both knew why he’d left. The marriage hadn’t worked, period. He’d been gone more often than he was with her, and she hadn’t been able to tolerate a relationship that was fitted in between SAS missions.

‘‘What makes you think things could be any different now?’’

‘‘I’m out of the military, and I won’t be going back. I don’t know if I can change—all I can do is try.’’

She wanted to be flippant, but the intensity of West’s gaze held her. He had never looked at her that way before, with heat and hunger and…need. She closed her eyes. ‘‘What if I don’t know what I want? What if I—’’

‘‘Want to experiment?’’

Her eyes flipped open. It had been five years, and in those five years she’d done a lot of growing up she didn’t know she’d had to do. She’d learned to reach for what she wanted, and she’d learned to say no. She’d been asked out on dates, and she’d gone out on a few—but never once had she been tempted to so much as kiss one of her escorts—or agree to a second date. The thought of any contact that was remotely sexual had filled her with revulsion.

She hadn't questioned just why she'd had zero interest in men, zero interest in sex. At first she'd had the trauma of the breakup to cope with, then she'd lost herself in her studies.

A prickling awareness ran all through her body, and panic knotted in her belly. She hadn't wanted to admit it could be because she'd never gotten over West.

She lifted her chin, and met his gaze. "What if I just want one kiss? No promises, no guarantees."

"Then take it."

He didn't move, and she realized he'd meant exactly what he'd said. If she wanted the kiss, it was up to her to take it.

She wound her arms around his neck and lifted up on her toes. Her breasts brushed his chest, sending a wave of heat through her. Her hips fitted against his, and the firm swell of his arousal made her belly clench.

He had always been lean and muscled, but now he was altogether broader than he'd been before, his shoulders wider, his biceps thicker, and his skin darkly tanned, with a seasoned sheen that said he'd been spending a lot of time in the tropics.

When they'd first been married, she'd read every bit of literature on the SAS and Special Forces she could find, in a bid to understand the man she'd married and the risks he was taking. The reading hadn't been reassuring—the statistics for relationships had been appalling—but it had been the graphically chronicled descriptions of past operations that had sent chills down her spine. When she'd finished her course of study, she'd had weeks of time alone to let the facts sink in. The next time West had come home, she'd *seen* him for the first time, the remoteness in his gaze, and she'd realized just how much of himself he kept from her. She'd wondered just which part of West had fallen in love with her—if he had fallen at all.

Taking a deep breath, she touched her lips to his. She breathed in, and tasted him, and emotion flared inside her, and she knew in that moment that she hadn't freed herself from him at all. If she had, she wouldn't want to touch him, she wouldn't want to be anywhere near him.

She'd had boyfriends before she'd married West. She knew what it was like when the relationship ended; she knew what it felt like to be indifferent; this wasn't it.

Curiosity and an almost forgotten recklessness, and something deeper—something hurt and tender—unfurled inside her. She pressed her lips more firmly to his, opened his mouth and delved inside. The liquid hot touch of his tongue sent a shock of arousal through her so intense that for long moments she was lost in the kiss, blank and clinging to West's shoulders—her body pressed so intimately close that she could feel every hard, shift of muscle, the slam of his heart, the rapid rise and fall of his chest.

West's leg moved between her thighs, his body eased up snug against hers, and she found herself turned and pinned against the counter, held there by heat and muscle, the press of his arousal, the taut stroke of his tongue.

His mouth on hers was hot, moving in a drugging rhythm that made her press closer still, arch and rub against him. He groaned, and a shudder ran through her. No one kissed like West—no one had ever touched her the way he did.

He lifted his mouth from hers, and bent to her neck. She felt the edge of his teeth on the tender skin beneath her ear, felt the rough drag of his stubble.

Delicious rills of pleasure spilled through her, and fear and panic knotted her belly. They could make love, and the thought electrified her. She didn't want to pull away—she didn't want to stop. On some mysterious female level she needed this. In the five years he'd been gone, she hadn't felt desire, and she hadn't missed it. When West had left, her sexuality had died as abruptly as her marriage, but now she felt like a dreamer waking up, her numbed senses flaring to painful life once again. In emotional terms she'd come out of deep freeze and was now being subjected to the heat of a blast furnace.

He lifted his head and his gaze locked with hers,

narrowed and glittering. ''If you don't want more, tell me to stop right now.''

Tyler blinked, for a wild moment she was tempted to lift her mouth to his again, slide her hands beneath his T-shirt and run her palms over the satiny skin of his back. The cool note of his voice registered.

He was giving her the opportunity to stop. She might have lost her head, but he hadn't; he was still firmly in control.

When West had left five years ago the lesson had been salutary. He was a loner. She had married him, but essentially she had never reached him—never held him. She doubted anyone could—then or now. The fact that he'd come back and seemed to want her again, didn't mean he had changed—it just meant she was repeating her mistake.

She should never have kissed him. Five years of training herself not to want West had just crashed and burned, all in the space of a few minutes.

Grimly, she pulled free. ''That's it—experiment over.''

She didn't understand him, and she didn't know if she ever would. He'd moved into her building because he wanted her back. If it was anyone but West, that kind of commitment would have shouted loud and clear that he was in love, and yet, essentially, he didn't seem to have changed. If he was in love with her, it was on a level she didn't understand.

She drew a deep breath, and let it out slowly. ''I don't understand why you're here. Why you didn't divorce me. You should be married by now. You should *be* with someone.''

''You made no move to divorce me.'' He said flatly. ''And if you don't care either way, then it shouldn't matter to you whether I'm married or single.''

''Well, I do care.'' He might keep his feelings under wraps, but damned if she would.

West's gaze sharpened. ''There hasn't been another woman.''

Tyler gripped the edge of the kitchen table and sat down. She stared at West in disbelief. ''Are you trying to tell me you haven't had sex in five years?''

His gaze locked with hers. ''What about you?''

''I haven't, either.''

Satisfaction glowed in West's eyes. ''That's one less man I have to kill, then.''

As men went, West had always looked sexual. For lack of a better word, *hot* women swarmed around him like the proverbial bees around the honey pot. ''Why didn't you?'' she wondered aloud.

''I'm not injured, if that's what you're worrying about,'' West almost smiled.

Heat rose to her cheeks. From what she'd seen—and felt—he didn't have any problems in that area, and probably never would have. *''Why?''* she demanded loudly.

Something close to temper flashed in his eyes. ''Simple. I wanted you. If I couldn't have you, the hell I would sleep with anyone.''

Chapter 10

She was sunk.

West hadn't made love with anyone since he'd left her. He had remained celibate.

How was *any* woman supposed to resist that?

Tyler glanced at the digital clock on the bedside table. Exasperation and frustration welled. She felt like punching the pillow. If her fingers weren't still bruised and sore, she would have.

It was five o'clock in the morning, and some time over the last thirty-six or so hours she had turned into a crazy woman.

She wanted her husband.

How dumb was that? Her marriage had been dead, with only the paperwork remaining to be seen to, and now all she could think about was what it would be like to slide back into bed with West.

If she slept with him, they'd be stuck together, literally for better or worse, for another two years before she could obtain a dissolution.

She stared at the slow, circling ceiling fan, and felt a strange, sneaky undercurrent that felt suspiciously like happiness bubbling up inside, filtering through the layers of fear and stress—the slow-burning rage at the attacks on her.

She couldn't remember the last time she had actually felt happy. Since West had left, she'd worked single-mindedly to attain her masters degree, then her doctorate. At first she'd buried herself in study, filling every moment of her days and her nights with research documents and technical publications—finding comfort in the academic world—then she had simply worked, and the habit of working long hours had stuck.

She glanced at the clock again. Any hope she'd had of getting to sleep any time soon was fast evaporating. She'd slept most of the previous day, and now she was wide awake, her mind running around in circles.

The moments in the kitchen when she'd kissed him replayed through her mind, and desire flooded her in a hot, achy wave, so that she turned on her side, curled her knees up and hugged her arms around her breasts, but the comfort of the fetal position didn't help.

If she was honest, she would admit that she would have slept with him anyway—before he'd told her the celibacy bit. It had only been a matter of time; now he was irresistible.

Pushing the covers back, she jackknifed out of bed, wincing when her head gave a warning throb. She waited out the ache, then moved more sedately as she pulled on her jeans, opened the bifold doors and stepped, barefoot, out onto the wet terrace. The sky had cleared and was tinged with a translucent gray in the east, and the early-morning air was soft and fresh after the rain. The wall rimming the perimeter was a deep line of shadow encircling the apartment complex, and the huge pohutukawa tree the attacker had climbed looked dark and mysterious, outlined as it was by the glow of the streetlamps.

A chill skimmed her spine. The men who had mugged her last night, and the man who'd broken into her apartment tonight, had gone to a great deal of trouble for crimes that hadn't netted much in the way of commodities. The mugging had seemed reasonably straightforward, although decidedly eerie because they had preplanned enough to knock the power out, and they had neglected to snatch her handbag when they could easily have taken it. If she was completely pragmatic about tonight's break-in, the man who'd broken into her apartment had to have been a rapist, and possibly a murderer as well. Why else would he make such elaborate preparations? If he simply wanted to steal—with his skills—he could empty apartments during the day when the owners were away at work.

There was only one answer that fitted. It was the same man and had been all along. He'd rung her up, followed her, then he'd taken his stalking a step further and had begun attacking her.

Tyler gripped the edge of the railing. Why this was happening to her now, on top of the trauma of the jade theft, she couldn't fathom. Whoever was stalking her was frighteningly organized, and an expert at breaking and entering.

He'd been wearing night-vision gear.

A shudder swept her. He had observed every move she'd made, playing a cat-and-mouse game as she'd inched out of the bed and felt around in the dark for a missile to throw at him. When she'd flicked the light on, he'd already been slipping out of the window, and the glass she'd thrown had missed him by a mile. Somehow, the cold calculation of his actions was more frightening than the mugging had been.

As reluctant as she was to let West any further into her life—as mystifying as he was to her—she was fiercely glad he was here. Despite the unsettling charisma, the potent sexuality, there was an unshakable calm to West that was at the very bedrock of who he was. When she was with him she was safe: it was that simple.

West set the phone back on the receiver, shut down his laptop and sat back in his chair.

Every instinct he had was telling him that something fishy was going on. The attacks on Tyler were too close to the robbery of the jade.

He'd left phone messages for Blade Lombard, Carter Rawlings and Ben McCabe—all three of whom he knew were in town. Blade, an Australian, was presently resident in New Zealand. Between changing diapers and breaking horses, he ran the Lombard Hotel and Casino. Carter, who was still on active service, was home on leave. Ben McCabe, another ex-SAS soldier, was now a security consultant in Auckland.

Blade, Carter and Ben were three of the best friends he'd ever known—and he had damn few friends. They, along with Blade's older brother, Gray, and his cousin, Cullen Logan, had all served together in the SAS, fighting in every corner of the world.

If West had family, this was it: the men he'd fought with. To call them friends didn't quite cover it. They were more like brothers than friends. When he'd first joined the SAS, he'd been as touchy and aloof as a wild animal—a misfit in the regimented world of the army, and more suited for the edgy world of Special Forces than anything else, but they'd simply ignored his keep-out signs and had worn him down with friendship.

There was an old Native American method of breaking wild horses called walking them down. They had walked him down. He'd known what they were doing, and he'd been powerless to stop the process.

After years of being more comfortable with isolation than company, they had bombarded him with cheerful camaraderie. He would sit at a table in the mess hall, and suddenly find himself surrounded. The banter had been nonstop, the jokes terrible. They had even touched him—when most soldiers took care not to touch him. He'd found himself nudged awake in the mornings with a booted foot, prodded in the chest, and casually slapped on the shoulder.

They had included him in their group until, finally, he was one of them.

He sat back in his chair. Amusement tugged at his mouth. They had even taught him how to tell the bad jokes.

West picked up the cats that had taken up residence on his lap and deposited them on one of the soft leather armchairs. He collected a spare pillow and blanket from the hall cupboard, and made himself comfortable on the couch. Within minutes both cats were climbing over him, investigating the best places to sleep. Tiger tucked herself into the curve of his shoulder, and the stripey male sprawled on his chest and settled down to purring. At least the cats found him irresistible.

West eyed the stray, whose head was situated only inches from his chin. ''You and me, huh?''

If this didn't work out with Tyler, at least he'd have company.

* * *

Tyler woke to sunlight pouring through the glass doors, and two cats sleeping on the end of her bed. Her little fluff-ball, Tiger, was curled up with the stray.

She reached out and stroked Tiger's silky fur. "So you decided to come and keep me company after all."

Tiger and the stray both lifted their heads, stretched, jumped off the bed and ambled in the direction of the kitchen. Tyler smothered a yawn as she eased out of bed. She checked the clock as her feet landed on the cool smoothness of the hardwood floor.

It was mid-morning. After lying awake for what had seemed like hours while the sun had risen, she must have drifted off to sleep, but the extra hours of rest had done her good. Her head felt clear, and close to normal, albeit still tender where she'd been hit, and the stiffness in her back and neck had completely disappeared. The only real evidence that she'd been hurt was the bruising on her knuckles, which was now spectacular, but contrarily, most of the stiffness was gone, so that she could bend her fingers without pain. That meant she could use her computer.

She walked through to the en suite and turned on the shower, running a mental list of everything she had to do that day as she undressed and stepped beneath the warm water and began lathering her hair—working carefully around her stitches.

First of all, she needed to get some more clothes

from her apartment, then see about having an independent alarm system installed. She no longer trusted the system that covered the apartment complex. It had been bypassed—easily—twice in two days.

After that, she needed to go into Laine's.

Just the thought of walking back into Laine's made her stomach tighten, the tangle of emotions wound through with a thread of anger. After days of being vulnerable and off balance, she had finally got some perspective on what had happened—and was still happening.

First of all, the robbery of the jade was not her fault. West had said that Cornell believed her to be innocent. The relief of Cornell's support aside, the jade had been as secure as any other artifact in the vault. She didn't know what had gone wrong. All she knew was that the jade wasn't in her possession, someone had taken it, which meant the security system as a whole was at fault.

Secondly, whoever it was who had taken it upon themselves to stalk and terrorize her wasn't going to succeed. In the light of day, she was more furious than afraid, and she was no longer alone.

The press was an annoyance, but she'd never placed any credence in anything that was printed before, and didn't see why she should start now.

Tyler stepped from the shower, dried herself, put on her bathrobe and walked back into the bedroom to change.

The fact that she was a liability with Laine's remained. Business credibility was one problem she would have difficulty solving. She might still have to leave, but she would wait before making a decision. Laine's was more than a career and a business for her. If she left, it would widen the gulf between her and Richard and Harrison, and that was something she didn't want to happen; they were her family.

Tyler went still inside, let out a breath and sat down on the edge of the bed, suddenly unsteady. She blinked. A tear rolled down her cheek, then another.

It was crazy, but in the middle of one of the worst times of her life she had found what she'd been searching for since she was eight—that magical, comfortable sense of belonging in a family. A family that was slowly drifting apart.

When Louisa was alive, she'd been the hub, but since she'd died, other than the occasional dinner together, the only contact they had as a family was at Christmas and New Year. Maybe if there were children involved, they would have been more inclined to spend time together, but in this instance they were all single; there were no babies, no kids, to pull them all together.

The problem was, they had no center. When Harrison wasn't working, he spent most of his time with his head buried in a book, and Richard wasn't much different—although his vice was computers.

If anyone was going to pull them all together, it would have to be her. *She* would have to be the hub of her adoptive family. Long minutes passed while she absorbed the implication and the concept that Harrison and Richard needed her beyond her capacity to work for the business. It was a strange, heady feeling.

Sunlight, hot on her back, broke her reverie, and reluctantly she got to her feet and began sorting through her suitcase for clothes. She needed to go into her office, if only to show her face and check on her messages—and she needed to go shopping and buy another laptop. She still had the disk with the information she was working on. She didn't know how useful the database she'd compiled was, but at this point she didn't know what else she could do to help. Cornell had tied up all the information within hours. He had the security tapes, and he had the vault log book, which was a simple manual register of everyone who accessed the vault during the day—a back-up system for the security cameras that worked around the clock, and the security personnel who were rostered on to administer access to the vault.

She hadn't seen either the tapes or the book, but Harrison had said they hadn't proved conclusive—that in fact, according to the security tapes and the personnel, no theft had taken place—which was why her position was so shaky. The jade was missing, and the fact that they hadn't found any evidence of a hard entry, made it highly likely that it was an inside job.

Her laptop was gone, but she still had her disk so

she could continue compiling her database of possible purchasers of the jade. Richard would lend her a computer until she bought another one.

She dressed for work, pulling on a loose white blouse and choosing a lime-green skirt that ended midway down her thighs because the shoes that went with the skirt were low and comfortable and she didn't want to risk a flare-up of the back pain. Normally, she wore her hair up for work, but there was no way she was going to be able to bear that, so she left it loose, blow-drying it and brushing it until it swung silkily below her shoulders. The outfit was softer and more feminine than the suits she normally wore, but still crisp enough for Laine's.

The apartment was still and quiet as she started down the hallway, and for a moment she wondered if West had gone out. A flash of movement caught her eye, and she paused at the door of one of the sunlit bedrooms, which had been converted into a minigym.

West was working out on a padded bench, wearing dark track pants that rode low around his hips, his back to her as he moved fluidly through a set of crunches; muscles bunched and slid beneath skin that gleamed with sweat and glowed gold in the morning light.

He had always trained, pushing himself to keep fit and build muscle for the strenuous assault work he'd done with the SAS. His dedication and commitment to his job had always been absolute, the habit of training a daily ritual that had closed her out as effectively as if she'd become invisible.

The memory on the heels of her vulnerability when he'd kissed her last night made her go cold inside. She could feel herself pulling inward, protecting herself like a turtle retreating into its shell.

Living with West had been like a crazy roller-coaster ride. When they'd been together she'd been his focus, and the intensity and passion that had flared between them had been overwhelming. He would walk in the door—tired and unkempt—lay his gun case down and shrug out of his pack. His gaze would lock on hers and every brain cell she owned would dissolve into slush. She would walk into his arms, lay her mouth on his and time would stop. More often than not, he'd still smell of gun oil and sweat and jungle, but it didn't matter. She never knew how long he was back for, or when she'd lose him next, and they'd spend most of his leave in bed.

Making love with West had been like heat and fire and magic combined, the pleasure so extreme sometimes she'd felt as if she were dying. Sometimes, West had seemed so absorbed in her, so completely lost in lovemaking, she'd fooled herself that he'd felt the same way she had, but he hadn't.

Despite all of her efforts to forget West, she hadn't succeeded. Like an injury that was too tender to touch, she'd simply covered this particular wound over, and it hadn't healed. Now she felt as if the layers had been peeled away, leaving her exposed, the sense of loss as sharp and fresh as if it had happened yesterday.

She'd thought before that, when it came to relationships, her loyalty wasn't in question, just her sanity: now she knew it.

She was still in love with West.

Chapter 11

Tyler blinked. For long seconds she couldn't think, couldn't feel. Then grief welled, holding her motionless when she knew she should be moving, and soon—otherwise West would see her. In that moment he sat up and turned in one smooth motion and his gaze locked with hers.

Her heart pounded in her chest, and her mouth went dry as he flowed to his feet and padded toward her. Without the civilizing barrier of a shirt, and with his dark mane of hair clinging to his damp shoulders, he looked big and male and dangerous, his exotic looks hammered into a tough maturity that made her stomach clench. Her stomach tightened with renewed tension when she realized that he was aroused, which meant that he'd been turned on *before* he'd realized she was watching him.

He came to a halt in front of her, heat poured off him, engulfing her. His gaze bored into her, his pupils so dilated they were completely black, and she knew in that instant that his control was almost gone and he didn't like it one little bit.

He cupped her face with his palms. "You should have kept walking."

His head dipped, his mouth closed hungrily over hers, and this time he wasn't playing the gentleman.

Long seconds later, he lifted his head.

Tyler drew in a breath and resisted the urge to step into him, wind her arms around his neck and press her mouth to his throat. "Was that supposed to be a threat?"

His gaze was hot, focused on her, and the pressure of his intent sent a shiver skimming down her spine. "You're better."

"Pretty much."

His gaze flickered over her office clothes. "Where are you going?"

His attitude said, Where do you think you're going?

"Work."

"The hell you are," he said mildly.

She lifted a brow. The blunt pronouncement after all the rocky emotion grounded her with a thump. West had always been a mystery to her, but this she understood. He was male, and he'd decided he was in charge of her. It was familiar territory. "You can't stop me."

"Put it this way—if you think you're going anywhere without me, think again."

She took a breath, let it out slowly. In the past two days, West had rescued her, acted as a buffer with the police, organized medication for her and stayed in her apartment so she'd feel secure. She knew he'd been concerned, protective, even proprietorial, but now she realized it was more than that. "You're acting as my bodyguard."

"I won't see you hurt again. You've been through enough." He bent his head and kissed her again, his mouth lingering, softening into a slow seduction that made her toes curl.

When he released her mouth, her eyelids slowly lifted. "I wasn't trying to get rid of you."

His gaze searched hers, abruptly cool and remote, as if looking for a rebuff, then she realized it wasn't remoteness at all, it was loneliness.

Tyler stared dazedly back at West, riveted by the emotion he wasn't making any effort to hide, and some of the disparate pieces of the puzzle that was Gabriel West clicked into place.

It registered that he *had* changed, but in all the years they'd been apart one thing hadn't altered—he had remained married to her.

In this day and age, maybe the concept bordered on the archaic, but for Tyler, the honor and purity of those vows mattered. She had married for love and she had married for life. Maybe she was naive, but she'd shied away from the thought of West becoming intimate with another woman, and she was fiercely glad he hadn't, that despite everything that had gone wrong, in this way she *had* held him.

She might not have fully understood what she'd had in a husband, but now she knew the only thing that mattered was that he was hers, and he had been ever since she'd walked into the nightclub where they'd first met eight years ago.

His hands settled on the wall either side of her head, he bent and his mouth fastened on hers, pressed her lips apart. His every action was slow and carefully deliberate. He was giving her time to move, time to back out.

When she didn't move, his breath shuddered against her lips, and his tongue slid into her mouth. Adrenaline pumped, and for long seconds she could barely breathe, barely think, her whole being centered on the slow, measured stroke of West's tongue, the sharp, building ache that quivered and burned through her. Her hands drifted up over his stomach as she lifted into the kiss, opening her mouth more fully. Her palms brushed the tight hard points of his nipples and suddenly she found herself pinned against the wall, his body moulded tightly to hers, the hard ridge of his arousal digging into her belly, sending a raw shock of excitement through her. Her arms wound around his neck, and a shudder rolled through him.

She felt his hands at her blouse, the impatient tug as he parted the lapels, the sound of fabric tearing.

She felt her bra loosen, the faint abrasion as the lace was pushed out of the way, then his hands were on her breasts, and she almost moaned with relief, they felt so tight and achey. He dipped his head and took one nipple in his mouth, drawing her in deeply, and the breath stopped in her throat for long dizzying seconds, her skin flashing hot, then cold as she struggled to cope with the swamping force of the emotions that flooded her. It had been years since she was touched intimately, years since she had felt the barest flicker of arousal, and now she was burning up, her skin so sensitive every nerve ending felt stripped bare. It was all she could do to stay on her feet; her legs so wobbly they felt like noodles.

His mouth slanted back over hers, hot and hungry as his hands slid beneath her blouse and cupped her naked back, arching her into him so that her breasts flattened against his chest. Abruptly, the burning heat of his skin, the sheer intimacy of what they were doing, sent a bittersweet shiver through her, and tears squeezed from beneath her lids. Her fingers wound in his hair, gripping him tight, and she felt the way his muscles bunched and shuddered at her touch. She wanted to tell him how much she'd missed him, how lonely she'd been—how much she'd missed this—because they'd never been closer than when they'd made love.

She felt cool air around her thighs and realized her skirt was pushed up around her hips. She felt a tug, and registered the glide of her panties as they slid down her legs. A muscular thigh moved between hers, and she moaned, arching at the rub of hot muscle, the texture of fabric against her sensitive skin. His hands closed on her bottom, and she clung to his shoulders as he lifted her.

Abruptly, she felt the prod of his sex parting her folds, and shock froze her as his fingers tightened their grip and the pressure between her legs increased as he began penetrating her, until, with a sharp shove, he was inside her.

For an endless moment, her mind went blank.

He was inside her already, the penetration deep, unexpected because, while he'd been fully aroused, only seconds had passed since he'd kissed her. She was aroused, but barely damp, all of her nerve endings quivering as she struggled to accommodate him.

He withdrew and slid into her again, and she arched, shivering at the burning lash of pleasure, the heavy intrusion, a part of her mind still reeling, disoriented. West was still wearing his track pants, and she was still fully clothed, apart from her panties. He hadn't bothered to remove her clothing, or his—there hadn't been time, he'd simply pushed fabric out of the way. Her skirt was still rucked around her waist, and her blouse hung open, damp and clinging to her arms.

His hands tightened on her bottom, settling her more firmly against the wall, one hand slid up her back and cupped her nape, supporting her as he began to thrust. She wound her legs around his hips, the movement tilting her pelvis so that he seated more firmly inside her, the deeper penetration sending waves of pleasure through her. He dipped and his mouth fastened on hers and heat exploded inside her. She felt weak and dizzy and breathless, the sultry weather squeezing all the air from her lungs, and she wondered that she'd ever thought she could forget this—that she'd ever thought she could live without him.

West's body was tight against hers, pinning her to the wall. She ran her palms over his slick chest, and his gaze flashed to hers, hot and glittering. His chest expanded and he shoved deeper, and excitement ran through her. This time she lifted to him, shivering at the thick length of him, the deepness of the penetration.

He bit down on the tender flesh at the apex of her neck and shoulder, and she climaxed, spasming around him, the grip so tight the sensation bordered on pain. She heard his muttered curse, felt his abrupt withdrawal, then he shoved deep again, and she felt the hot pulsing spill deep inside her.

Long minutes passed while they lay limply against the wall. Her face was buried against his neck. She could feel his breath stirring through her hair. Her clothes were tangled and tight, and where skin touched, they were glued together by heat. She could feel West's heart slamming in his chest, echoing her own unsteady heartbeat. She could feel him hardening inside her.

The hot, stirring ache started again, and her belly clenched. She lifted her head. His gaze caught on hers, held, and she drew in her breath at the softness there.

"I could make you pregnant."

She considered what it would be like to have West's child growing inside her, and her chest squeezed tight. For years, she'd shelved the whole need to have a child, but now it hit her like a fist. A baby. A child. She felt sensitive and shaky. Maybe because she'd had such a traumatic childhood, ever since she could remember she had wanted children of her own, wanted to cuddle and hold sweet-smelling babies. Logic and practicality didn't come into how she felt, especially with West naked inside her. She wanted a baby. Her gaze lifted to his. "Is that a problem?"

His chest rose on a sharp intake of air. A dark flush rimmed his cheekbones. "No," he said from between clenched teeth, and he swung her into his arms in one fluid motion. "No problem."

West carried her through to his bedroom, not stopping to remove their clothes. The weight of him settled on top of her, and she drew an unsteady breath as he slid slowly into her, the heavy glide deep and slick and deliciously smooth, the penetration deeper than before. This time, the lovemaking was prolonged and deliberate, saturated with the knowledge that he'd come inside her once, and he was going to do so again.

This time when she climaxed it was hot and slow and sweet, and when he came inside her, he held her tight against him, pulsing deep into her womb, the moment bathed in heat and curiously suspended as they drifted into sleep.

She woke by slow increments. Her eyes flickered open. The room was stifling, the day's heat building, pressing in on her so that even breathing was an effort. Big purplish clouds obscured the sun, making the light yellowish and murky, and signaling the onset of another heavy downpour. The bedroom clock said it was late afternoon, but even the knowledge of how much time had passed while she'd lain twined with West wasn't enough to rouse her.

West was sprawled asleep beside her, his arm heavy across her waist. Where they touched, the heat they generated sealed their skin together, but she felt sleepily content and unwilling to move.

Thunder rumbled in the distance. Warm, damp air drifted into the room, laced with the scent of ozone, and it began to rain outside, a slow heavy pattering that seemed to increase the steamy heat.

West stirred beside her. His hand moved across her belly, his palm hot and callused against her sensitive skin, and her heart thumped in her chest.

He could make her pregnant, and the thought both elated and alarmed her. She was twenty-eight, and she had only ever fallen in love once, and she now knew herself well enough to know that this was it—this was her man. The thought should have panicked her, but she felt oddly serene. She hadn't set out to have unprotected sex, but it was done now.

She turned her head on the pillow to find West watching her, his eyes sleepily intent.

He climbed off the bed and eased his track pants off, then began systematically removing her clothes. When he was finished, he lay sprawled beside her, basking in the heat like a large relaxed cat. One lean finger traced the line of her cheek, and then he began to play with her hair.

Sleepy as she was, she could feel herself responding to his lazy touch. His thumb stroked over her jaw. A delicate shiver ran through her, and she turned into his arms, wrapped her arms around his broad back and buried her face in his neck, breathing in his warm, heady scent.

She'd meant to go to work, to get an alarm put in, and instead she was lying naked with West, and they were spending the day in bed making a baby. After the years apart and the painful process of their marriage breakup, she should have been panicking—at the very least questioning her decision—but oddly, she felt more settled than she had felt in years.

She ran her fingers down the deep groove of his spine, enjoying the sleek maleness of dense muscle and smooth skin, the slow building anticipation as she lifted her mouth to his.

His face was half in shadow, half out of it. "Again?"

This time when he slid inside her, she felt exquisitely tight and sensitive, every nerve ending tingling and almost preternaturally alive. She could feel herself sinking, drowning, the intensity building slow and sweet and piercing, until, when her body locked tight and he poured himself into her, she had the strangest idea that they dissolved together.

The next time Tyler woke, the long afternoon twilight had darkened into early night, with the rain still falling in solid sheets, and the air temperature cooling. West turned on lights, fed the cats, made a pasta dish that they ate in record time, then he pulled her into the shower with him. When the water went cold, they toweled dry and slipped back into bed, although it wasn't late.

For an indeterminate period they simply lay entwined, listening to the rain and dozing, neither inclined to move more than was necessary.

West's hands moved lazily over her, his touch slow, exploratory, building a slow, restless tension that kept her from sliding into sleep. Tyler started her own exploration, sliding her hand down over the ridged line of his lean belly to his genitals. She cupped him, feeling his instant response as he stirred in her grip. Like the rest of his body, this part of him was beautifully made, the shaft long and thick, his testicles heavy.

She smoothed her palm over West's chest, dipped her head into the shadowy curve of his neck and shoulder. On impulse she opened her mouth over the taut curve of muscle. He tasted male, faintly salty, and utterly delicious.

His sleepy gaze sharpened. "You bit me."

"You didn't like it?"

For an answer he drew her hand to his mouth and bit down on the soft pad of flesh beneath her thumb. A raw shudder went through her.

His mouth curved in a slow, easy grin, riveting her attention as he lay back on the bed and propped his arms behind his head, watching her. "You're so dominant. You get on top."

Tyler swept hair back from her face, drawn by his grin; the invitation to play irresistible. She felt giddily happy, almost dizzy with delight.

She didn't know how she'd got here, but suddenly she was in completely new territory. She was head over heels in love with the stranger who just happened to be her husband. He wanted her, he'd just spent most of the day proving how much, and crazy or not, they had just bound themselves together in the oldest way there was, by trying to make a baby.

West's gaze caught hers and held. Her heart slammed hard against her chest, and for a moment she had difficulty breathing. West was strong. She'd always thought of him as invincible, never as vulnerable, but suddenly her mind was filled with the crazy notion that maybe West was just as vulnerable as she was.

Chapter 12

Tyler spent the next day working on West's laptop reviewing the information she'd collated on disk and trying to add to it. An officer from the police department rang asking if she needed counselling after the mugging and the break-in. Tyler resisted the urge to say that what she wanted was an arrest, and hung up.

Late in the afternoon, she went back to her apartment, checked all the rooms and packed more clothes. When she walked back into West's apartment, he was working on his computer.

She placed the suitcase she'd brought on the floor, feeling edgy and unsettled because even in broad daylight, she hadn't felt safe in her own home. "I'm going to ring around and get some quotes on a security system."

"You don't have to worry about that. I've already asked Ben to come around and install a system."

"Ben as in Ben McCabe?"

"He's the best in the business. And besides, he's a friend, he'll give you a discount. If you've got a problem with that, I can put him off."

"No, no problem." Except that Tyler remembered Ben from the years she was married, *actively married,* to West, and it felt odd that he should come around to do the security. In a strange way it was almost as if her past life was reconstructing itself around her again.

West closed down his program. "Cornell rang. They're broadening the jade investigation. They think that whoever broke in here might be connected with the theft."

Tyler let out a breath, not knowing whether to be relieved or terrified. After days of being out on a limb with the police, the press and Laine's, suddenly she had support. The crimes still didn't make any kind of sense—even less so when all grouped together—but if a cold, competent player like Cornell believed, then some kind of concrete link must exist.

West rose from his seat. "I've been putting some feelers out to contacts in Interpol. Did Cornell take both sets of security tapes?"

"Along with a third back-up set that Richard keeps."

"So that leaves the computer system itself. If it's

an inside job, that's the only place we can start looking. Do you still have keys?''

Tyler extracted the keys from her purse.

''Then let's go and see what we can find.''

She checked her watch. It was five-thirty now, still sunny and light outside, but Laine's would have closed. ''I'll ring Harrison and tell him what we're doing, then I'll call the night watchman and tell him to expect us.''

Laine's was quiet as Tyler keyed in her PIN and waited for the lock to disengage. Above her she was overwhelmingly aware of the surveillance cameras, their presence overt and a little daunting, even for customers, but a necessary measure. Since the jade had been stolen, the auction house had lost clients. If they lost many more, the business would be hurt. In order to keep some shred of credibility they had to be seen to have impeccable security. The building and all entrances and windows were now under twenty-four-hour camera and manual surveillance. If so much as a sandfly moved, the security team would know it.

The door swung open and they stepped through. West glanced around the lobby as Tyler closed the door behind them. ''Pretty cameras. Who did the job?''

''ALC Security Systems. Harrison's dealt with them forever.''

''Good solid firm.''

She met his gaze. "But what?"

"I don't have a problem with ALC. In fact it'll make what I'm going to do easier. They're an old firm—very straight line—which means they'll do things strictly by the book. That means no smart-ass young kid's been in there and created a reputation for himself with oddball system writing." His gaze skimmed the hushed carpeted interior of the auction rooms as they moved through the building. "That's probably why you got ripped off. Someone saw the opportunity and manipulated your system."

"So we lose, no matter how good the system is."

"With computers, it's always a crap shoot. The technology's moving so fast, security can't be assured."

Tyler pushed open the door to the office where the junior staff worked and the computers that were linked into Laine's network were kept. She sat down and booted up the system. "Cornell's had ALC's experts going through the system. What do you expect to find that they can't?"

"Maybe nothing, but there's no harm in looking. It's possible that ALC will be blinded by their own programming. I won't be. I also have the advantage that I didn't write the program, and I don't need to stand by it."

Tyler keyed in her password, then accessed the security program. "The whole vault is wired. Whenever anyone opens a deposit box the computer logs it and allocates a number. That means there's a numerical sequence for every action that involves the use of the deposit boxes. A separate system screens the vault door. The security guard checks each person in, and writes the computer-generated number into the manual log book. At the close of business the vault is time-locked until eight the next morning, so no one has access at night.'' Tyler stood and moved back so West could sit down. ''As a system it was supposed to be foolproof.''

West scrolled through the menu. ''What happens if the power shuts down?''

''The telephone system automatically pages our security firm, and they dispatch a crew. In any case, the night watchman is here. If he thinks anything is even remotely suspicious, he calls the police and whichever manager is rostered on to do after-hours duty.''

West's fingers moved across the keyboard. A new screen popped up. ''How often are the deposit-box numbers checked?''

''They're not checked unless there's a problem. The only staff allowed in the vault are managers. That's a total of eight people, including Harrison, Richard and myself, and we're each accountable for our own stock. Until now, the system's worked perfectly.''

West began generating reports for the day of the robbery, his gaze moving quickly across the tabulated columns on the screen matching names, dates and times with the lists of figures that represented deposit boxes. He swore softly. "All the figures run in sequence, but that doesn't mean much when the jade's gone. Either the thief disconnected the entire system, which would mean a security call out, or he got into the program and rewrote it so that what we're looking at here isn't reality—it's whatever he, or she, wanted the program to show."

He called up another menu and was stalled when the program denied access. His gaze settled on hers. "Who has access to the software?"

For a moment Tyler went blank. "In theory, no one."

"Who?"

Tyler drew a breath; her stomach churned sickly. "Richard's the only person I know who's had anything to do with the system. He worked with ALC to design it."

West exited the program. "In that case Cornell will have it covered. If Richard worked with ALC, they'll be hauling his ass across the coals as well."

"It's not Richard," she said bluntly. "It can't be."

West got to his feet, his expression noncommittal. Richard Laine was wealthy and successful, but his personality was essentially sealed off. In that respect, they were similar, but in every other way they were as different as night and day.

With the value system that West had evolved as he'd moved from the brutality of the streets to the discipline of the military and the refined savagery of the business world, there were certain absolutes that had stuck. Loyalty and honor among them. But, in the final analysis, everyone had to stand in their own power. Whether he was on the street, in a battle situation or a boardroom, West knew that kind of self-sufficiency when he saw it. Tyler had it in spades. The first time he'd seen her, he'd recognized the quality. It wasn't anything tangible—just there. Richard, wealthy and supported by a loving family as he was, had never needed that kind of strength.

The absence of strength didn't make Richard a criminal, but it did make West watchful. Until he *knew* Richard he would remain watchful. "The perp could be anyone who has access to your computers, and who has a good understanding of your security system as a whole."

"Then we're back where we started. With nothing. The thief could be anyone."

"Not quite. Now we know the thief is a computer buff. And I'm willing to bet he's tampered with the camera footage, too."

The next morning, Tyler took a seat at West's desk and moved the mouse on the pad. The screensaver flicked off, and she stared blankly at the message that was still on the screen. There wasn't much to it. The message was addressed to West, and was an agreement to meet in an hour. The person who had sent the message had simply signed himself as Chen.

West had left just minutes ago to attend a business

meeting with Blade and Gray, but hadn't mentioned that he would also be meeting a Chinese contact.

Tyler wasn't sure what West was up to, but she was almost certain the meeting wasn't business, and that it had something to do with the jade theft.

Tyler began searching West's mail directory, skimming systematically, but there was no reference to the mysterious Chen.

Chen could be anyone, the reasons for West to be meeting with him, manifold. He could be an expert in Chinese jade, but if Chen was legitimate, why hadn't West brought her and the police in on the meeting? And why keep it from her in the first place? The only reason she could think of for the secrecy was if West was meeting with a source who *wasn't* legitimate. It was even possible that Chen was a member of the Chinese underworld.

A chill went down her spine. She knew West had spent time in China both for his work and privately. The fact that West had spent much of his childhood and adolescence on the streets and had known all the gangs and a large percentage of the criminal underworld didn't do anything positive for the equation.

That West was trying to help she didn't question. It was the *way* he was trying to help that worried her. The publicity attached to the jade was explosive; it had damaged her business credibility, and the media had already linked the two of them. If they decided that West had anything at all to do with the jade, they would be merciless.

She went still inside. She was worrying about West's connection to the theft of the jade, but that aside, if the press decided that West was seriously close to her, they would go for his jugular anyway.

As yet, the fact that she was married, but separated, had only been touched on by the media, but with West firmly back in the picture, it wouldn't take long for the press to drag out all the details they could on the early part of his life. Her background had been dicey enough—West's had been savage.

Maybe he had a good reason for the secrecy. Whatever his reasoning was for taking the risk, she couldn't condone it. The jade had been stolen from Laine's. It had been stolen from *her.*

She hit the disconnect on the e-mail, picked up the phone and rang Maia, who had been coming to "baby-sit" her in West's absence, and put her off, then she walked quickly through to West's room. *Their* room, she thought, her stomach turning a somersault as she grabbed her handbag, checked that her car keys were in the side pocket and, on impulse, rummaged in her suitcase for a scarf.

Fifteen minutes later, Tyler located West's car in the car park of Lombard's Hotel, parked a discreet distance away and sat, air-conditioning on full blast while she waited. Less than five minutes had passed before he strolled to his car, slid into the driver's seat and nosed out of his space. She followed, hands damp on the wheel as she tried to keep at least two cars behind him. Luckily, her car wasn't glaringly distinctive. It was a light bronze color that was popular enough that it blended with the stream of traffic, whereas West's car was dark enough to stand out.

She recognized the route long before they reached the destination. West was driving to the airport.

She followed him into the car park at a snail's pace, keeping her distance—noted where he'd parked, and drove into the next block of spaces, pulling in beside a dusty pickup truck that would completely obscure her car from West's field of vision. She grabbed her handbag, locked her car and peered around the edge of the truck. At that precise moment, West looked almost directly at her as he pushed dark glasses onto the bridge of his nose. She ducked back out of sight, heart pounding for long tense seconds, half expecting West to walk around the side of the truck and ask her what she was doing following him.

She counted to five, then looked again. West was walking toward the terminal building: he hadn't spotted her.

Letting out a breath, she grabbed the scarf from her bag, hooked the handbag over her shoulder, and tied the scarf peasant-style around her head as she threaded her way through the cars. The scarf was a piece of indigo silk she'd bought simply because she'd liked the deep color and the supple quality of the silk. It wasn't much as disguises went, but it was dark enough that it wouldn't draw the gaze. Most important, it hid her most distinctive feature, which was her hair.

She waited until he was almost at the terminal building before she started after him, only to have to duck down behind a car when he stopped at one of the parking-ticket booths.

It took something away from the clandestine nature of the thing for West to calmly get a parking ticket before he undertook whatever illegal or undercover activity he was engaged in. Of course, it was always possible that this wasn't where he was meeting the mysterious Chinese person—he could be here for another entirely mundane reason, and the meeting place was elsewhere.

Gritting her teeth, she decided that she would have to get her parking ticket now also. Otherwise, she'd be stuck with getting a ticket when it was time to leave, and if she wasn't careful she could lose him altogether.

She tossed up whether she should just calmly walk to one of the machines and feed her money into the slot, then decided against the idea. The booths were open and exposed, all facing the large windows that fronted the terminal building. The likelihood that West would spot her was too great. She would have to wait until he'd obtained his ticket and entered the building, which meant she could lose him completely.

Frustrating seconds passed while he waited in line. When he finally moved away from the booth, Tyler walked briskly to the nearest machine, slotted coins in, obtained her ticket and tucked it into the pocket of her jeans as she walked through the glass doors and into the departures foyer. She skirted the long, barnlike building, trying to stay merged with groups of people. When she didn't see West anywhere, she took the elevator up to the next level, the one with shops and cafés, avoiding the escalator because that would expose her to view on both levels for too long. After doing a brief circuit of the retail area without spotting West, she finally settled on the vantage point of a bookshop, which gave her a good view of the area, including the escalator, with the added bonus that she could hide behind a book if she did see West.

Minutes later, she saw West's distinctive figure. He was strolling with an exquisitely dressed Chinese man. They stopped in front of the café adjacent to the bookshop, shook hands, then the Chinese man walked rapidly away. Instead of leaving, West strolled into the bookshop, and picked up a newspaper.

Tyler moved behind a bookstand, her heart thumping. She counted to ten then peered around the bookstand, to check where he was, but he had disappeared.

''What in hell are you doing here?''

The book Tyler was holding flew out of her hands. She spun around and almost bumped into West's chest. Her heart stopped, then pounded back to life.

"What do you think you're doing?" She bent and retrieved the book and put it back on the shelf.

"Trying to figure out what you're doing."

Tyler could feel herself flushing, the color rising in a hot, swamping tide. "I was making sure you were all right."

"Why wouldn't I be?"

"I thought you might be setting up a meet with some, you know..." Now that she had to say it out loud it sounded ridiculous. "Some Chinese bad guys."

"Triad? You've got to be kidding."

"He wasn't Triad?"

"Chen's too busy minding his own assets to try and steal anyone else's. If he wants a company, he takes it the legal way, but he does collect jade. He's going to see what he can find out about the theft in the Asian community. I didn't want you involved in this because Chen can work better without being publicly linked with Laine's. It's a delicate matter. Chen also happens to deal in jade and he has an intimate knowledge of all aspects of the jade market—including the black market. On more than one occasion he's had to track down pieces, but for him to do the work he needs to be discreet. If he's coupled with this scandal, it'll scare off his sources."

West's hand dropped to the small of her back and she found herself propelled forward. "Just out of interest, how did you find out I was meeting him?"

"I read your e-mail."

"You read my e-mail." He shook his head. "Why didn't I see that one coming?"

He took her hand as they threaded their way between the café tables, and pulled her toward the exit.

Tyler scanned the swirling mass of people and saw the notice they were attracting. "What if someone takes our photo?"

West said two succinct words. "It'll give them something else to talk about besides the jade."

She tried to unlink her fingers from his. "I don't want you linked with me in the papers."

He stopped abruptly, keeping his grip on her hand, his gaze dark and enigmatic, and the vulnerability she'd only guessed at surfaced again, taking her breath. "You're worried about what the press is going to do to *me?*"

She nodded. "Hard to believe, huh?"

A slow smile started in his eyes. "Honey, the second I went into partnership with Lombard's the press took a chunk out of my hide. They think I'm a gangster. Come to that, they think Blade and Gray are gangsters."

Tyler stared at West blankly. He was utterly relaxed about what the press could or could not do to him. She felt relieved and irritated at the same time. It was illogical. After all the worry she'd invested on his behalf, the lengths she'd gone to to protect him, she should feel happy that West, and his business, were impervious to the press. "Were you ever worried—?"

"Not in this life."

"—because, damn it, I *was.*"

He grinned, slid his hands around her waist, and eased her close. Smoldering irritation aside, she could feel herself dissolving. She should scream, she should yell for airport security and *ensure* they got their photo in the paper. With her publicity track record, one more scandal wouldn't even register. "Buddy, you're dicing with death."

"I like walking the edge." For a split second his grin widened, then she lost her perspective as he bent his head and laid his mouth on hers.

Her heart stopped in her chest, then pounded back to life. He smelled clean and male and tasted like soda, and the kiss was so good it was indecent. He shifted his mouth and she could feel herself drifting deeper. The hum of conversation, the low-level hustle and bustle of the airport receded, and abruptly she remembered how it had been last night—the sheer warm intimacy of sleeping with West again. She had felt safe when, under normal circumstances, she should have lain awake most of the night reliving those moments in her bedroom when she'd known someone was there.

West lifted his head, as if he'd felt her tension, and a faint shiver skimmed her spine at the watchfulness of his gaze. For a moment she'd almost forgotten that essential part of him—and that he'd met Chen to try and get a lead on the man who was stalking her.

When he'd gone after the intruder the previous night, for the first time she had seen how he was in battle. His face had been the face of a hunter, blank and cold and utterly focused. In love or not, she would be crazy not to remember who West was—*what he was*—and that West not only liked walking the edge, he loved it.

West untied the scarf where it was knotted beneath her chin, let the silk fall around her shoulders and ran his fingers through her hair. "Since you've already had a taste of undercover work, I've lined up another assignment tonight. According to Blade and Gray the Lombard Casino has recently become a prime stamping ground for one of Laine's managers."

The casino was full, the floor and the bars a cacophony of light and sound and pulsing color.

In an adjacent bar, a band was playing a blues number, and the husky wail of a singer and the sensual murmur of a sax wove smokily through the packed floor.

West kept hold of Tyler as they paused to buy chips, not because he thought she was in any danger here, but because Tyler was certifiably gorgeous in green silk, and the casino was filled with males on the prowl. He was damned if he'd allow any other guy to think he could make moves. He handed Tyler a packet, then guided her toward the tables.

She slipped the chips into a beaded evening bag

that matched her shoes, *and* her underwear. The dress she was wearing was sexy to keep him on edge all evening, what she had on underneath made him break out in a sweat.

She slung the strap of her evening bag over her shoulder. "You're not going to gamble?"

"I've done enough gambling to last a lifetime. I don't need the roulette wheel."

"If you're talking about your job, then you're right," she said curtly. "Every time you went away on a mission *was* a gamble."

"It was never a gamble. I knew I'd be okay."

West went still inside. He'd never voiced it before, but that's exactly what he had known, that he wouldn't die or be seriously hurt. He'd worried that he was losing it mentally with the risks he'd been taking, but a part of him that he seldom acknowledged until he was actually in a battle situation had *known* he wasn't taking a risk. He could label it prescience or clairvoyance, whatever, there was nothing too weird in it, although most people would see the experience as borderline. West knew that Blade was psychic. He also knew that Blade would personally break every bone in the body of anyone who pointed that fact out—except, of course, his wife. Anna could tell Blade he was an alien from Mars and he'd purr like a pussy cat.

Relief loosened a tension inside him that he didn't often recognize, or even put a name to. He wasn't certifiable, then. The psychic talent he possessed had simply worked in a way he hadn't expected. He'd had a premonition. Although in his case it hadn't been about something bad happening; he'd had a premonition of safety.

Tyler squeezed his hand. "What's wrong? You look as though you've seen a ghost."

West focused on Tyler. He hadn't seen a ghost, but he'd laid one to rest.

Carter strolled past the slot machines and joined them.

West lifted a brow. For Carter, dressing was simple: jeans, boots, T-shirt and gun. It wasn't often he could be coaxed into any kind of formal gear. Tonight he was wearing dark trousers that had a faint silky sheen, a white collarless shirt, and he'd finally invested in a jacket. "You got a jacket to fit."

Carter's gaze skimmed the floor. "Had to get it made."

"About time. Where did you go?"

"Not to that little dive off High Street you recommended, that's for sure. That place was full of stockbrokers and wedding dresses."

"DiVaggio's showroom."

"That's the place. There was a tall, dark guy in there. Gave me the creeps."

"Gino Veronese. DiVaggio's floor manager. Hell of a retailer."

"I don't care who he is, or what he's selling, I'm not buying."

West's mouth twitched. He lifted a hand, acknowledging Gray, who was walking toward them. "Couple of years back he tried to date Blade. That only happened once."

"I'll bet. Speaking of Blade, where is the Prince of Darkness tonight?"

Gray came to a halt beside Carter. "Probably upstairs changing diapers. It's his turn."

A dark form materialized on Tyler's right, making her start. She caught the edge of a white grin, the unmistakable line of Blade Lombard's profile.

"These days it's always my turn. Anna's pregnant again." Blade traded a look with Gray. "I've been checking the floor. We've got unexpected company." He nodded in the direction of the blackjack table.

Gray's expression remained unchanged, but his gaze was icy. "They won't be staying."

A slight Chinese male dressed in an exquisite suit approached, coming to a halt several feet away, he was flanked by a second figure, dressed completely in black. West recognized the suit was Li Chou, number-three son of the infamous Chou family, which operated out of Hong Kong. Li was the head of Australasian operations. He spent most of his time in Sydney—it was unusual for him to be in New Zealand at all. The protection was Kim Soon, one of the Triad's top hit men.

He met Kim's impassive gaze and shifted to shield Tyler. At the same time he became aware that Carter, Gray and Blade were flanking him. All around, the hum of conversation continued to flow, twined with the smoky blues number, but the tension was palpable enough that an area cleared around them, leaving a pool of silence.

The greeting when it came was soft, formal, the bow slight, but respectful—open hands, showing the palms. No weapons, a messenger only. Li Chou extended the politesse to include the Lombard brothers, the ritualistic formality of his gesture acknowledging the raw burn of power in the air. Beneath the exquisite tailoring of evening dress, Gray and Blade were both armed: this was Lombard territory. West caught the subtle shift of movement, noticed the smooth positioning of Lombard security. If there was trouble, the odds weren't good for the Triad.

Gray and Blade both acknowledged Li Chou, and ignored Kim. West replied in Cantonese, matching Li's formality.

The message was short, succinct. "We have no business with Gabriel West or his family." The bow acknowledged Tyler.

"What about Laine's?"

Li's gaze flickered to Tyler, an uncharacteristic hint of surprise giving emotion to his still features. He directed his reply to West. "Laine's is your family. Naturally, they are under your protection."

West controlled his own surprise at the way in which Li had couched the relationship. For some reason Li and the Triad families were presently regarding him as the head of Laine's. The message was both obscure and crystal clear—as close to a declaration as he could ever hope to get that Triad, and Triad interests, had nothing to do with the theft of the jade. Not that that was a big surprise—the theft had been slick, but the mugging had been sloppy. Triad wasn't sloppy. If they needed to steal anything, or carry out a hit, they sent a professional, like Kim.

Tyler stepped forward, ignoring West's restraining hand. "You're talking about the jade. But if you had done business with Laine's, you would have transacted the business with me, and I don't know you."

The silence stretched, the tension gathering, coalescing until it was thick enough to slice.

This time Li's bow was curt, almost non-existent. "We do not deal in jade."

Tyler watched the men return to their table, a little shudder running down her spine. She regularly dealt with Asian clientele and was used to the difference in manners and body language, the ritualistic etiquette involved. Their being Asian had nothing to do with her reaction. She liked her Asian clients, but this guy was certifiably creepy. "Who was that?"

"That," West said grimly, "*was* Triad, and you just broke the unbroken rule."

She suppressed another shudder as she watched the innocuous little man with Li bend down and hold a lighter to the businessman's cigarette. "What rule?"

"You made him state what he was really talking about."

Tyler turned her attention to West. "I know just where he can stick that rule."

"The little guy with him is Kim. Now there's your Asian bad guy. He's a killer."

"He doesn't look lethal."

There was a small silence, then West's hand settled at the small of her back and Tyler found herself propelled toward the exit. "I'm getting you out of here before you insult any more people."

West nodded at the security guard at the door. "Kim doesn't want to look lethal because he doesn't want trouble with the cops."

"I just asked him a question. How was I to know they were Triad? It's not as if they wear a tattoo on their foreheads—"

"They're organized crime. These days it's a multinational business. They deal in drugs and money laundering. Trust me, the people who need to know they're Triad, know."

"Including the police and Interpol."

"You've got it. They run legitimate businesses. Li is the CEO of a manufacturing conglomerate. He exports computer components out of Taiwan. The motherboard for your laptop probably came out of his factory."

"So, if he's Triad, and supposedly invisible, why did he expose himself like that?"

The glass doors slid open, the abrupt change from air-conditioned coolness to the steamy warmth of an

Auckland night instantly made her skin prickle with heat.

"The publicity of the jade theft has put the spotlight on the Asian underworld, and Cornell's been a busy man, he's been applying pressure. That was the Triad's way of saying ease off."

"And you're supposed to tell Cornell to back off?"

West's shoulders lifted. "Cornell's doing his best, but police resources are limited. Why look where the jade is least likely to be?"

The roulette wheel spun, the raucous sound gradually winding down to a series of rhythmic clacks as it slowed.

A man detached himself from the noisy, jostling crowd pressing in close around the wheel before the marker found its final resting place. Coldly, he skimmed the crowded floor, taking in the flamboyance and the noise, the tourists rubbing cheek by jowl with the addicted poor and the jewel-bedecked wealthy.

Over the past ten years, he'd systematically robbed some of the wealthiest homes in the Pan Pacific region, always keeping to his area of expertise—diamonds—and he'd amassed a tidy fortune, although he'd been careful to keep the bulk of his wealth offshore. He had a Swiss bank account, a block of apartments in Paris and a lavish property in Geneva.

Over the years, he'd created a number of identities

for himself. Traveling under different passports allowed him to move freely in the countries he was working, without jeopardizing his legitimate identity and his job with Laine's, both of which allowed him an inside track on who was buying expensive gems, and provided the ultimate cover. After all, who would suspect a diamond buyer, working in one of the toughest, high-security jobs outside of Fort Knox, of moonlighting to steal the merchandise he traded in?

The diamond business was tightly regulated by the major diamond players—the gems allocated on a drip-feed system into a hungry market in order to keep the value sky-high. It was a seller's market, often by invitation only, where even the buyers themselves were screened. Credentials were everything, and dealing for Laine's put him in at the top end of the bidding and set the seal on his credibility.

He had been repeatedly screened every way a person could be screened short of a full body search. His security rating was the highest. When he walked through international borders with a briefcase cuffed to his wrist, he was escorted by bodyguards, on a priority pass—first-class all the way.

The irony of the security buzz around him, when he was one of the bad guys, never failed to amuse him.

Chapter 13

The underground car park was reasonably well lit but decidedly dim after the lights of the casino. The car was parked some distance away. Normally, Tyler didn't mind the walk, but the dimness brought back the eeriness of the mugging in the car park.

A footfall sounded, soft and distant. Tyler's breath dammed in her throat despite the fact that West was with her as she waited for the next sound—and didn't hear one. She couldn't remember if she'd heard the doors to the hotel slide open or not—but she didn't think so. And no vehicle had driven in; therefore the person who had made the noise had to have been already in the car park. That didn't mean that the person had a suspicious motive for being there, though; it was possible they were simply waiting for someone.

The sound came again, closer this time.

West cursed softly beneath his breath. His arm came around her waist, and she found herself pulled behind a pillar.

His breath was warm and damp in her ear. "Wait here."

The seconds stretched out, amplified by the utter silence in the car park. Outside, she could hear the hum of city traffic, the distant wail of a siren. Tyler heard a surprised grunt, a brief scuffle. When she peered out from behind the pillar, West had the man who'd been shadowing them pushed up against a car.

The man West had caught was medium height and broad-shouldered with a short haircut that made him look ex-army. As Tyler walked slowly toward them, West abruptly let the man go.

The shorter man straightened and reached gingerly into his jacket to extract his wallet. "My name's John Leland. I'm a P.I. My firm also does security work. I was hired to follow Miss Laine and take note of all her contacts, and to intervene to protect if necessary."

"Offensive surveillance."

West perused Leland's photo identity. Leland hadn't lied. He worked for one of the smaller security firms in town.

He handed the card back. "Who hired you?"

"Richard Laine."

West slid his arm around Tyler and pulled her close to his side. He wasn't sure of the legal ground—it was a gray area unless the security firm actually did intervene in Tyler's life—but technically, Tyler wasn't their client. "Tyler hasn't agreed to any kind of surveillance or protection."

Leland's face reddened as slipped his wallet back into his jacket pocket. "You weren't supposed to know about it. May I have my gun back now?"

West slipped the confiscated Browning from the waistband at the small of his back, took the magazine out and handed the unloaded weapon back to Leland. He then emptied the magazine into his pocket and handed him the empty magazine. Damned if he'd have Leland following either him or Tyler out of here with a loaded handgun, no matter who had hired him.

A quiet footfall sounded behind them. West turned to see Richard walking toward them. His gaze narrowed. He hadn't seen Richard inside the casino, but that wasn't so surprising; the place had been packed.

Richard nodded at Tyler, then met West's gaze. "I hired Leland because I didn't trust you to keep Tyler safe."

West had no problem with Richard's bluntness, or the fact that Richard didn't trust him to look after his sister. If he was in the same position, he'd be just as wary. "Call him off," he said softly.

Richard's gaze was cold. "Or what?"

"Or you'll have Cornell to contend with. What you're doing isn't legal."

Richard went white, then nodded curtly at Leland.

Tyler watched as Leland walked a short distance

away, got into a late-model sedan and backed out. She glanced at Richard. ''How long's he been watching us?''

Richard looked sheepish. ''About two hours. This was his first night.''

She closed her eyes briefly. ''You should have asked me.''

''If I'd asked, you would have turned the offer down, and I wanted you to have some kind of protection.''

''I've got my protection. In case you didn't notice he managed to neutralize *your* guy in about ten seconds.''

Something hot flashed in Richard's gaze, and suddenly he didn't look wary or cold or uncertain, he just looked angry. ''It's not my area of expertise, but I had to do something. Someone's playing games, and I don't know if the police can nail him because he's damned slick. I've been searching Laine's database for the bastard.''

Tyler's throat went tight. "That's what you've been doing?''

Richard's jaw squared. ''What did you think? That I was just working late? That I'd let you get beaten up, or take the blame for the theft without doing anything to help?''

Tyler swallowed. ''I didn't think that.''

Richard let out a breath. ''The theft was an inside job. Someone got in and rewrote the program. The new version date is the day the jade was discovered missing.'' He shoved a hand through his hair, suddenly looking distracted. ''We need to go to the office, but first I need to go home and get my laptop.''

Richard placed his laptop on his desk and flicked a lamp so that golden light pooled through his office. He plugged his laptop into the network computer that also took up space on his desk, and booted both systems. He grabbed an extra chair from a neighboring office, and motioned both Tyler and West to sit down, then dumped a pile of CDs on the desk.

''I've developed a search engine that's adapted to searching files, documents, e-mails—anything that can be stored on computer. All I need to do is key in certain words and it'll queue the documents in priority of the most hits.''

He placed a zip file on the table next to the laptop. ''I've had the program running twenty-four/seven for the past week, so that every document that fits the parameters and that's online for even a nanosecond gets copied.'' He grinned, looking faintly sheepish. ''Including all e-mail.''

He sat down and began keying through menus. ''That's why I've been working late. I've been spending hours every night sorting through garbage.''

He punched in a command, and within seconds a list of several hundred documents accrued. ''Those are today's hits.''

West eyed him sharply. "How did you learn to do this?"

Richard clicked on the first document and began skimming it. "I play with this stuff in my spare time. It's a hobby."

West watched him scroll through the pages. "I've done a little programming, but I prefer designing hardware."

"So I heard."

Richard met West's gaze and West's stomach relaxed. Whoever the thief was, Richard wasn't involved. They might have their differences, but they were all to do with experiences, not bedrock qualities like honesty and integrity.

Richard picked up a CD and fed it into the computer. "Ninety-nine percent of the stuff I've been catching has nothing to do with the jade that was stolen. I've stored everything that *is* directly connected with the jade on this disk. Every piece of documentation, every bit of correspondence and all of the security records from the initial transaction when we secured the pieces is on file."

He hit a button, and the original purchase document for the jade came up on the screen.

Tyler ran her eye loosely down the screen, scanning the information. The name on the purchase order and receipt was Kyle Montgomery. Something clicked into place in her mind. Kyle had stepped in and done her job as a stopgap measure after the previous manager had left, and while she finished her doctorate. He had bought a house lot of estate jewelry and auction goods, which had included the jade, but he hadn't understood the significance of the find. Months later, when Tyler had taken over, she had examined the jade and brought in an expert who had identified the pieces as very fine quality Sinkiang nephrite, and the entire world of ancient artifacts had gone wild.

Reuters and CNN had picked up the story, and it hadn't taken long for the sheer mystery and the human-interest angle of finding the personal effects of a warrior monk, predating the Shaolin, in amongst Maori grave goods, to overtake the exquisite rarity of the find. The artifacts, and Tyler, had become front-page news. The fact that Kyle had made the original purchase and had failed to understand just what it was that he'd bought had never been mentioned, and Tyler, aware that artifacts were not Kyle's area of expertise, had deliberately kept that information under wraps.

When Richard moved to scroll the screen, she stopped him. "Have the police interviewed Kyle?"

Richard looked thoughtful. "They've interviewed everyone who had access to the vault, which includes Kyle."

She moved the cursor on the document until it came to rest on the name of the purchasing officer. "Kyle made the original purchase of the jade, but he didn't know what he'd bought."

Richard clicked on the print button. The machine

hummed to life and a copy of the document slowly fed out. "Lately, Kyle also likes gambling. That's what I was doing at the casino tonight, keeping an eye on him."

He passed the copy to West.

West's expression was cold. The link was sketchy, but right now even sketchy would do. Aspects of the theft had been accomplished by someone who knew Laine's security system intimately. Kyle Montgomery had had the access, and he had known how the security worked.

The only thing missing had been motivation. If Montgomery had a gambling habit, that was a powerful motivation to obtain a lot of money, fast. It all still didn't add up for West—something was missing—but they had enough to get Kyle taken in for questioning again.

Richard's fingers tapped restlessly on the desk. He picked up a pen and scrawled the receipt number on his blotter. "That number. It rings a bell. Hang on."

He began sorting through the discs, sending them scattering before finally selecting one. He removed the previous CD and slipped the new one into the slot, then began searching.

Abruptly he stopped. "This is it. I don't know what it is, but it's something. It uses the first four digits of the receipt."

West read the brief e-mail which consisted of nothing but numbers and letters. He leaned closer, every instinct on full alert. "That's a map reference.

And that,'' he said, pointing at a set of letters and a number, ''is a motel.''

He glanced at the original receipt of the jade. ''Bingo,'' he said softly.

Someone who preferred to remain anonymous, was using the original receipt number for the jade as a reference.

Chapter 14

The jade bird nestled in the palm of his hand, the largest of the primitive artifacts surprisingly heavy for its compact size.

He lifted a glass to his lips, inhaled the smoky perfume of forty-year-old whiskey, savoured a mouthful, and let the potent liquid slide down his throat. The liquor burned in his belly, reminding him that he hadn't eaten since breakfast, and now it was late afternoon.

He set the tumbler down on his coffee table, beside the other two pieces of jade and contemplated smashing them all.

All in all, he didn't know what the fuss was all about. The nephrite was a pretty shade of green, but the material was heavy, opaque and oily; he much preferred the translucence of jadeite.

His mouth curved grimly. Come to that, what he really preferred were diamonds.

Resisting the desire to toss back the rest of the whiskey, he flipped his briefcase open, wrapped the jade in thick pieces of velvet and wedged them in beside *her* laptop.

He grinned, remembering what it had felt like to take the briefcase off the bitch. On impulse, he took the laptop out, flipped the lid and booted it up.

She was back with her husband.

A tendril of anger slid past his control. That was a contingency he hadn't planned for. He'd watched her to make sure she was isolated and alone, and he'd made sure she was hurt and frightened. Gabriel West intervening hadn't been a part of the equation.

In retrospect, he'd made a mistake in hitting her in the garage, but he'd been so incensed that she'd fought back at all that he'd struck out.

Hot blood coursed through his veins at the memory, throbbed in his groin. He picked up the tumbler and allowed himself another sip, nursed along another pulse of excitement.

He had nearly had her the other night.

He should have had her. The cycle should have been complete.

His fist closed on the glass, and it broke, so that the remains of the whiskey leaked through his fingers along with a thin trail of blood.

Distantly, he watched the pinkish liquid soak into

the carpet, and analyzed the physical effect of the small stinging cut.

Pain was an interesting tool. It could heighten pleasure, and it could take it away.

The broken pieces of glass dropped to the floor with a faint tinkle, and with abrupt, precise movements, he shut the computer down, closed the lid and placed the laptop back in the briefcase.

Broodingly, he went over everything he'd learned about Gabriel West. His knowledge was frustratingly little for the amount of effort he'd expended.

The man was garbage—scum—but he was physically dangerous. He knew that, as much as he'd trained and honed his own martial arts skills, he couldn't compete one-on-one with West.

Excitement shot a cold thrill up his spine. He'd probed and prodded into the military world, but the SAS were a close-mouthed bunch, and he'd had to be discreet. He had managed to get a few snippets of gossip from an army private, but the details had been blurry. West came and went, he'd spent a lot of time overseas, and he was regarded as some kind of god when it came to weapons.

He also had powerful friends. The Lombard family, of all people.

He strolled to the liquor cabinet, tipped another measure into a fresh glass and took another sip, savoring the smoky bite and frowning at the hollow feeling in his belly. He needed to eat, but right now the last thing he felt like was food.

He had to move, and move fast.

He picked his cell phone up off the coffee table and punched out a number. When he got an answering service, he terminated the call without leaving a message. One of the things he was careful never to do was to leave a tape recording of his voice, anywhere. He also never used his home phone for any "business" calls; preferring to use a cell phone that could be discarded in an instant.

His jaw tightened as he strode into his study and sat down at his computer terminal. It was Saturday—Reed should be at home. He typed out a short e-mail and pressed the send button. When the message had gone, he picked up the cell phone and tried the number again.

Richard dropped his briefcase on the floor in his office, set his container of Chinese take-aways on his desk, and sat down at his keyboard, almost forgetting the food as he touched the mouse to refresh his screen, then slipped the disk he'd brought with him in the zip drive.

He'd set up a program that searched service providers. The program, nicknamed Ferret, acted like a virus, but it was very subtle, and so far had eluded virus scans. Ferret reacted to specific words and word groupings. When it registered a hit, it e-mailed the post to a temporary address Richard had set up in an empty office in Newmarket. It was highly illegal, but very effective. The program was also ultra-high risk;

the applications strictly for clandestine operations. If he could sell the technology to the CIA or the FBI, he'd be a wealthy man.

If his bug was found and traced, he would be in trouble, big trouble, although he'd done everything he could think of to protect his rear. He'd rented the office under an assumed name and paid cash. The e-mail address was a free one, again purchased under an assumed name.

Committing computer crime, he'd found, had been ridiculously easy, but if he didn't hit anything interesting in the next twenty-four hours, he would terminate the program.

Richard pulled the zip file directory up onto the screen and accessed the contents. He set the screen on a steady roll, flipped the lids on his take-aways and sat back—chewing on egg fried rice and cashew chicken as he skim-read the messages.

Despite the risk in violating a supposedly secure mail system, and his anger at whoever was jerking Laine's chain, for the first time in years he was having fun.

He'd worked in the family business since he'd left university following in his dad's overlarge footsteps, and he was comfortable there, but computers had always been his passion.

He read a section of an e-mail that was definitely X-rated and grinned and shook his head. Knowing what he did, he would never risk broadcasting his love life over the Internet.

A familiar word grouping caught his eye. He dropped his fork, spilling rice onto the keyboard, and scrolled back until he found the e-mail.

He uttered a short sharp oath.

The address wasn't the same, but the content almost mimicked the message they'd found two days ago. Whoever had sent it had changed their address, but the message had appeared anyway because the wording was basically the same—the only difference was in the date and time.

Richard dumped the take-aways down on the desk and picked up the phone.

West sat back in his chair, keeping his gaze on his computer screen as he picked up the phone.

''Our man's online again,'' Richard said tersely. ''He's changed his tag, but elements of the message duplicate.''

Tension coiled in West's gut. This was a break none of them had expected. The odds that their man would e-mail again, using any of the same elements, had always been a long shot, that they could locate the message had bordered on the impossible.

''And, West, he uses a number. I checked to make sure, and the numbers are the last four digits of the receipt used on the original purchase of the jade. I think he's still got the jade and he's setting up a buyer. If everything runs to schedule, we've got an hour and a half.''

West swore softly. ''I'll give Cornell a ring.''

''I'm coming over,'' Richard announced. ''Whatever you do, wait for me.''

The phone clicked in West's ear. His mouth curved ruefully as he stabbed in Cornell's cell phone number and waited for him to pick up. Against all the odds, he was beginning to like his brother-in-law.

Cornell's answering service came on line, which meant Cornell must be on duty and busy. If he was at home, he would have picked up. West left his name and number, then tried Farrell's number. When Farrell's answering service kicked in, he left the same brief message.

A quick call to Auckland Central netted zilch. The duty officer at Central sounded harassed. It was Saturday night, and the place was crazy with nightclub brawls, domestics and kids racing their cars on city streets. There was a shooting in West Auckland, an Armed Offenders Squad callout in Remuera, and to top it off, someone had climbed the Auckland Harbour bridge and was letting off fireworks up there. If Cornell made it back into the station at all, he would be surprised. Farrell and a number of other officers were locked into the AOS operation. How long that would take was anybody's guess, but even if it was all over in minutes, they would still be delayed at least an hour by the AOS debrief. He would page Cornell, and try his car radio, but he couldn't promise anything. The second personnel became free they would be dispatched.

West tried Cornell's number again. When there

was still no reply, he called Carter. If the message Richard had intercepted was correct, they had an hour, max, to make the meet. If Cornell or any of his team turned up, they would step back and let the police do their work. If the police didn't show, then the hell West would let this go. They'd worked hard, and against all the odds, they'd gotten a break.

Carter picked up almost immediately. When he heard West's voice, he grunted. "This better be good. It's the third quarter and we're losing."

West could hear the football game playing in the background. "Sorry if I'm breaking anything up, but I need you. If it's the NLR game, I already know the score—I caught it on Sky. You can cry on my shoulder when you get here."

Carter said a short, sharp word.

West grinned and gave him the details of the meet. "You can take out your frustrations with some undercover work. Get Blade, if you can."

"You've gotta be kidding. He'll probably get there before I do."

Half an hour earlier. He examined his reflection in the mirror. Time for a change.

He unwrapped the package he'd brought, and set the peroxide and the hair color he'd bought down on the bathroom counter and picked up his bleaching cap. Systematically, he pulled hair through the cap, then applied the peroxide. When the peroxiding was complete, he rinsed his hair, dried it, then applied the color. While he waited for the color to fix, he worked on his eyebrows and lashes. When the coloring processes were complete, he threw the empty packaging in the bin, showered, and changed into black pants and a black cotton sweater. As he toweled his hair dry he critically assessed his reflection in the slightly misted mirror, then unwrapped his final purchase, and fitted colored contacts to his eyes. He slipped the case into his pocket and blinked until the lenses were comfortable, then stared at himself.

He walked back out into the lounge and placed the velvet-wrapped jade into a small cardboard box which was packed with foam padding, closed the lid and taped it with plain brown packaging tape. He snapped the lid of his briefcase closed, then walked through the house one last time to check he hadn't left anything behind that he needed to take.

He had already air-freighted most of the personal belongings he wanted to retain to an address in Antwerp, Belgium—under another false name. The rest of his belongings had been packed into plastic bags and taken to the dump. His luggage was loaded into his car, along with his travel documents—including travel insurance—all under a false name.

When he was in Europe, he frequently used one identity in particular for periods of time—accustoming himself to the persona, so that if he ever had to be Edward Hammel, an appraiser of fine gems, he could step into the role in a heartbeat.

Once he'd delivered the jade, and verified that payment had been made to his Swiss account, he would have no further use for his old identity. He would *be* Edward Hammel.

Chapter 15

Richard arrived at West's apartment with his laptop and was quickly followed by Carter and Ben. A few minutes later, Blade and Gray walked in the door.

West wasn't surprised to see Blade; if he so much as sniffed trouble, he was there—but he lifted his brows at Gray. Gray had spent years doing undercover work for the SAS and had specialized in jungle work, but he was now a family man and spent most of his time in Sydney, managing various facets of the Lombard empire. These days, he only made fleeting visits to Auckland.

Gray ambled over to join Richard in studying the e-mail that Richard had intercepted, their conversation low-key and relaxed. Gray and Richard were acquainted, because in the high-flying world of business in which they both moved, the social circle was relatively small.

Blade handed West a newspaper. ''Looks like your cover's blown.'' He tapped the caption beneath the picture. ''Says you and Tyler are the new Bonnie and Clyde of the business world. Anna's going to be ticked. That used to be us.''

West studied the photograph, which had been taken in Tyler's hospital room. Satisfaction curled through him when he saw that he'd been identified as Tyler's husband. That was useful because it would broadcast to the guy who'd been stalking Tyler that she was no longer alone. The stalker already knew that Tyler had a man around, but if he understood that he was her husband, he should back off altogether. Men who preyed on women and children weren't brave, they were just calculating. West was willing to bet that the stalker would think twice before he walked into a situation where *he* could be at risk.

The article also carried information about his days on the street, his SAS career, and the fact that he was now in partnership with Lombard's designing weapons and communication equipment for special forces. ''How in hell did they find out that last part? I thought that was classified.''

Blade shrugged. ''Ever since that fiasco last year with Ben and Roma, the press has been on our tail. If they don't have an earthquake or a war to report, they want to know what we're doing, who with, and for how long.''

He prowled restlessly around West's almost empty lounge, and stopped in front of the terrace doors, staring out at the deepening gloom that signaled another overcast night, with the promise of rain. ''Where's Tyler?''

''Having a shower.'' West handed the paper to Ben. The fiasco Blade was referring to had happened just months ago, and had involved the contract hit man who'd executed the oldest Lombard brother, Jake. The hit man had appeared on the scene years after the event to stalk Roma Lombard who was now Roma McCabe, Ben's wife. They'd caught Linden in the end, but not before there had been a storm of publicity.

Blade continued to pad restlessly around the lounge and finally perched on the arm of the couch.

Ben passed the paper to Carter. ''The article says you've reconciled.''

''For that he can live.'' West fastened a knife sheath to his ankle. He had a cold, edgy feeling in the pit of his stomach, a feeling he'd gotten used to when he'd gone on SAS ops. His instinct was to go for the spine sheath as well, but that was a little too anarchistic for Auckland—even on a Saturday night.

West noticed that Ben was openly carrying, using a shoulder rig that faded almost to invisibility against his black T-shirt; the holstered Glock as straightforward and uncomplicated as McCabe was himself.

When West straightened, Ben pulled several folded sheets of paper from his pocket. ''Sign that.''

West knew what it was before he looked at it. A protection contract that enabled Ben to carry his firearm on the street—strictly in the line of duty. He looked into McCabe's cold, blue gaze and knew what he was offering. If he had to shoot someone to keep both him and Tyler safe, he would do it. ''I don't have time to read the fine print.''

Ben handed him a pen. ''You don't need to. That's the part that says if you or Tyler get hit, it's not my fault.''

West scribbled his signature and handed the sheets back. ''What kind of protection is that?''

Ben grinned and pocketed the contract. ''The only kind you can get outside of a war zone.''

Carter tossed the newspaper down on the coffee table. He looked as restless and edgy as West felt. ''So...are you and Tyler back together?''

The tension in the room ratcheted up a couple of notches. Each one of them had steadfastly refrained from asking West what he was doing in an apartment in his wife's building when he owned a perfectly good house just minutes away. The answer had to be obvious, if a little extreme, but when it came to extremes he wasn't alone. West knew the lengths that Gray and Blade and Ben had gone to to get their wives and keep them safe. West met Carter's blue gaze. ''Not exactly, but I'm working on it.''

Carter didn't bother to hide his irritation. West

knew that Carter considered that he was as forthcoming as a sphinx when it came to talking about his relationship with Tyler, but West wasn't about to bare his soul. He'd spent a lot of time with these guys—they'd lived in each other's pockets for years. When they were on patrol it had gotten even more intimate than that because they'd had to survive in such close quarters and depend on each other to stay alive. There wasn't much about any of them that they all didn't already know, but for West, Tyler and his sex life—or lack of it—had always been off-limits as a topic of conversation.

"And?"

"And I think it's working, but she's driving me crazy. Is that what you want to hear?"

West checked the glittering edge of a blade, then slid the knife into the ankle sheath. He would pick up a handgun and a shoulder holster from his house. Going armed at all was a risk because he wasn't licensed to carry like McCabe, but in this instance it was a risk he was prepared to take.

"Jeez, I knew you couldn't forget her, but after all this time..." Carter shook his head. "That's why you've been—"

West shot him a warning glance. "Don't say it."

Blade rose from his perch on the arm of the couch. "Celibate."

So much for his sexuality being sacrosanct.

There was a moment of hushed silence. The kind of complete silence that falls when somebody gets seriously injured or dies. West supposed that something had died; it had been his libido, although it had never completely given up. He just hadn't wanted to have sex with anyone but Tyler.

Richard looked up from his computer. "Celibacy," he murmured. "That's hard to grasp."

Gray perched himself on the other end of the couch from Blade. "Don't even try, mate. Don't even try."

The sound of a door closing, and feminine footsteps, broke the faint tension, the male closing of ranks on a conversation that had prodded into the holy of holies—a man's sex life—abrupt and complete. A woman was coming.

West's relief was short-lived. He let out a breath when he saw Tyler. She was dressed in black jeans, a V-necked T-shirt that did bad things to his pulse, and black boots. Her hair was swept back in a ponytail, revealing the sculpted planes of her face. She looked more like a secret agent than any of them—the only mercy was that it was night and she couldn't wear sunglasses. West smothered a grin.

Oh yeah, he could see her in the sunglasses. Maybe he'd get her to wear them after this was all wrapped up and they were alone.

Her green gaze fastened on his. "You're not leaving me behind."

His grin faded. There was no question in her tone; it was a flat, hard-ass statement of intent. He didn't want her to come with them—it was too dangerous—

and he didn't want to leave her behind. In his view that was even more dangerous. The guy who was stalking her wasn't on the level. If Tyler was with him, at least he could keep an eye on her. "You can come, but you'd better obey orders."

Tyler grinned, suddenly looking more like a teenager than a twenty-eight-year-old doctor of anthropology. "Always."

West tried to look grim, and failed. They were on the edge of nailing the thief, recovering the jade and, if his suspicions were correct, catching the guy who'd attacked and stalked Tyler. Every time he thought about the mugging and the break-in—that damned night-vision gear—his stomach clenched and his jaw locked. He should be settling into battle mode—becoming distant, self-contained. That was what usually happened, but suddenly this whole thing was taking on the aspect of a school picnic.

Blade whistled approvingly. "Hey. Like the boots."

Tyler slung the strap of her bag over her shoulder. The bag matched the boots, naturally. "Kick-ass, huh? I got them at the September sales. If you give me your size, I'll look out for a pair for you."

Carter rose to his feet and shook his head. He'd been ready for the past half hour, but it was obvious he was out on a limb all by himself here. "While you're at it, look for a handbag for him."

Blade lifted a brow. "Ease up, Carter. Just because you've got a phobia about handbags."

* * *

As soon as West stepped inside his house, he became aware that something was different. Wrong.

He paced through the airy, high-ceilinged rooms. The house was a Victorian villa he'd bought as a doer-upper, an expensive old lady of a house that was all hard work and no fun without someone to share all the big empty rooms with. He'd sanded and polyurethaned the floors until the Matai timber shone with a high gloss. He'd scraped paint and replaced weatherboards, spent weekends building decks and making and fitting bifold doors to the lounge, family room and main bedroom. He'd built a large garage and workroom, put in a pool and dug gardens. He knew every inch of the house, every inch of the property. He knew how it felt.

The sense of wrongness persisted. There was no one here now, but someone had been in the house.

He strode into the large open-plan family room, his gaze skimming coldly over the television, video and stereo system. Everything was in place, nothing appeared to have been touched. He moved systematically through the rooms, then came to a stop at the cupboard under the stairs which he used as a gun safe.

As a registered collector of guns, he had to comply with strict security regulations with the storing and security of the firearms. When he'd remodeled the under-stairs room, he'd more than complied: he'd built a fortress. The room itself was lined with heavy timber and sheets of steel. The door was made of reinforced steel and had a computerized security lock as well as a heavy steel bolt. The bolt was still in place, but the padlock was missing.

Grimly, he retraced his steps to his bedroom, pulled on a pair of thin-skinned black leather gloves and returned to the gun safe. Carefully, to minimize damaging any fingerprints that might be on the bolt, he slid it back, then punched in his PIN to deactivate the lock.

The door swung open, he flicked on a light. The small storage room was lined with locked gun racks, cabinets for handguns, shelving for ammunition and his reloading equipment. All it took was one sweeping glance to see what was missing. The Bernadelli.

The bastard had stolen his favorite handgun.

Chapter 16

Cornell ducked out of the rain into the lighted portico of the town house, pushed the bell and waited. He had a search warrant in his pocket, two detectives from Central flanking him, and another four he'd pulled in from South Auckland who had closed in on the back of the property, covering all exits in case their boy tried to do a runner.

The door swung open.

Montgomery's gaze slid to the two uniforms behind Cornell. "What the hell—"

Kyle Montgomery was dressed for an evening out. Cornell decided it was an easy bet he was headed for the casino. He held the warrant in front of Montgomery's face and recited chapter and verse.

Montgomery continued to bar the doorway.

Cornell gauged the set of his jaw. "We can do this easy," he said flatly, "or we can do it hard."

Montgomery swore, and stepped back. "I'm calling my lawyer."

"You do that, Mr. Montgomery." Cornell motioned his men inside, keeping tabs on Montgomery in case he decided to bolt. "Just don't try to leave."

"Am I under arrest?"

Cornell stepped inside and closed the door behind him. "Not yet."

The motel was brightly lit, both flashy and anonymous. It was one of a popular nationwide chain, which suited his purposes; he didn't want a nosey private motel owner checking up on what was and wasn't happening with the rooms. It had the added advantage that it was within walking distance of his apartment, which meant he didn't have to use his car. The risk that the people he was dealing with might obtain his car registration and trace him was slight, but why expose himself needlessly?

He strolled across the car park, avoiding the well-lit areas, and turned in the direction of unit 31D, which he'd rented two days ago for the initial meeting with the team who were brokering the sale of the jade.

The men he was dealing with were an unknown quantity, but he'd picked them rather than deal with the recognized brokers of black-market gems and artifacts for the simple reason that he didn't want to deal with professionals and risk a trail that would lead back to him. Black-market brokers were solid to deal with; they had to be, otherwise they would end up in the bottom of a lake somewhere, but in this case, the pressure generated by the notoriety of the jade was too much of a variable to discount. Someone would talk. His primary concern now was to get rid of the jade as quickly as possible. The money was secondary. Reed was adequate, and if he fumbled the deal, he would simply write it off with the rest of this debacle.

He walked on to the attractive patio of the unit, turned the key in the lock and walked inside, flicking on lights as he went. He'd tossed up whether or not to go to the expense of securing the unit by paying for an entire week, or taking his chances that one would be available when he needed it—and had decided that that was one variable he wasn't going to mess with. It was summer and the peak of the tourist season. He was damned if he'd have to ring all over town looking for a motel with vacancies because he'd been too tight to pay the extra bucks. The rooms were stock standard, as Joe-average as the rest of the place, with the usual overkill of air fresheners and cleaners, but the units were very private, each enclosed by thick plantings of subtropical shrubs and tall, arching palms. They also had the additional advantage of three exits: front, back, and sliding doors in the bedroom.

He wasn't planning on having to make a quick

exit, but neither was he discounting that possibility. His plans had gone so badly awry since he'd first executed the robbery that he had to consider the possibility that more could go wrong.

His jaw tightened as he removed a framed print of a pastel still life from the wall, and accessed the wall safe—the other reason that had made this particular motel a desirable location for the transaction. He placed the taped box in the wall safe, returned the picture to the wall, then walked back out onto the patio, leaving the door ajar.

Glancing at his watch, he strolled across the graveled drive and unlocked the front door of the second unit he'd secured, directly opposite the first.

Gently, he closed the door behind him and locked it. Leaving the lights off, he walked through to the rear of the unit and unlocked and opened the rear door, leaving it very slightly ajar.

Returning to the lounge, he set his briefcase down on the dining table, flipped the lid and extracted the Bernadelli handgun nestled in beside the jade. He hefted the pistol and sighted down the barrel. The Bernadelli was primarily a sporting weapon, but this one had been customized for street use; the barrel shortened, and an ultra-sensitive trigger added along with a two-chamber muzzlebrake to allow exhaust gases to escape. In terms of street use, it cut down on flash and curtailed the kickback when fired.

He checked the clip. If he had to shoot one or more people he would. He had too much at stake to lose everything now. If the deal went sour on him, he would use the weapon to implicate West in the theft of the jade, and the murder of a person or persons involved in the sale of the artifacts. The charges probably wouldn't stick—West had powerful contacts—but they would muddy the situation enough to take any heat off his disappearance.

The way he felt right now, he was pissed enough that he would shoot someone anyway.

He parted the drapes just enough that he could see the warmly lit unit just metres away across the gravel drive, and sat down to wait.

West dialed Cornell's cell phone as he drove.

"Damn." He terminated the call. It was Saturday night—crime-wise, the busiest night in town. Cornell was probably tied down breaking up nightclub brawls and booking drunks.

He pressed Redial and handed the phone to Tyler. "Get Cornell or Farrell. Keep trying until one of them picks up."

He parked the car a small distance from the motel, which was located on a pleasant, mainly residential street just off a busy intersection. Blade and Gray, Carter and McCabe were already parked, waiting for them. Richard had volunteered to stake out the police station and grab the first detective available.

Tyler sat in the car and kept dialing Cornell while McCabe checked lip mikes and handed them out. Within seconds the five men had merged into darkness, and it had started to rain, moisture drifting down in slow motion, wetting the pavements and putting a glistening sheen on the palms. The low pattering of rain hitting the car roof and windscreen created a hypnotic, somnolent feel to the night.

Tyler absently watched the blinking neon sign that marked the motel entrance as she waited for Cornell to answer his phone. When his answering service came on line, she hung up and decided to call every two minutes. She checked her watch beneath the yellowish light of the streetlamp. It had only been five minutes since West and the others had melted into the darkness, but it felt like longer.

The rain intensified, drumming loudly on the metal roof of the car, muffling all exterior sound. The windows had fogged, making the luxurious interior seem smaller, claustrophobic, and making her feel even more cut off from West and what was happening at the motel unit.

She checked her watch again and let out a breath. The second hand was crawling.

Cornell's jaw set as he listened to the croupier at Lombard's give her statement that not only had Kyle been at the casino on the night in question, but she'd gone home with him when her shift had finished.

It seemed that Kyle's evident gambling obsession was a front for an affair. The pretty croupier had been seeing Kyle for the past month, and since she was married and was frightened her husband might use the evidence of the affair to contest custody of their child, they'd kept it quiet until she could get herself and the child out of the house and into the inner-city flat she'd just secured.

Cornell had already sent a detective over to Lombard's to impound the tapes, but he knew what he was going to find. Sweet nothing.

It wasn't the first time it had happened, and it wouldn't be the last.

He said a short, succinct word beneath his breath.

They had the wrong guy.

The air-conditioning unit in the darkened motel room hummed, pushing back the humidity of the rain-filled night, the low-level noise breaking the silence.

The man standing at the edge of the long drapes shrouding the front window shifted uneasily. He was shielded from the gaze of anyone who happened to peer out of the unit opposite, but he still wasn't happy.

He'd set up one previous meet with Elgan Reed under the same conditions. Reed had gone to the motel unit and waited until the phone rang. To Reed, he was just a voice over the phone, but it had given him a chance to study the man. He was nervy, a little uncertain. This was probably the first big deal he'd brokered, which made him a pain in the ass and perfect for the job.

If Reed and his couriers fumbled the ball and got

caught, then they were on their own. They wouldn't be able to implicate him because they had no idea who he was, and there was no way the jade could be traced back to him. Even if there was speculation that he might have been the perpetrator of the theft, then it wouldn't be his problem; he would be gone. After tonight, he would cease to exist.

He picked up his phone and pressed a short dial. Seconds later the motel receptionist came on the line and connected him through to the unit.

He watched as Reed picked up the receiver.

"What's going on—"

"The package is in the safe."

He gave Reed the combination.

Reed yelled for a pen and swore as he scribbled out the sequence, bitching that he hadn't turned up in person to make the transaction.

One of the men took the painting off the wall, dialed the numbers and opened the safe.

"Make the payment. If you try to leave the room before I've verified that the deposit's in my account, I'll kill you."

Reed's blustering trailed off. "Now, there's no need for that—" His face had gone pale and shiny with sweat. He swore beneath his breath. *"You're watching us."* His swallow was audible. "Where are you?" His gaze flitted around the room, fixed on the window in front of him, and he swore again. "Hold on."

Reed held the phone away from his ear and began

talking to his friends, his voice rapid as he stabbed a finger at the window.

In the same instant a shadow detached itself from the shrubbery between the motel units, and his eyes flickered with shock. He should have spotted anyone approaching the unit, but somehow he'd missed the movement, and even now he couldn't make the figure out clearly because whoever it was was dressed in black. The shadow moved again, and this time he caught the sharp edge of a profile—and a lip mike.

Adrenaline pumped, electrifying him. He'd been made.

He didn't know how it had happened, but the only reason for armed police to be here was because somehow they'd found out about the meet.

Gently, he replaced the receiver on its rest, picked up the gun and the briefcase, and walked out the back door.

West paused at the back-door entrance of the motel unit just as the door burst open. Two men careomed into him, one catching him full in the chest with a package. The momentum shoved all the breath from his lungs and slammed him back against the wrought-iron railing that bounded the small deck. His gloved hands closed in automatic reflex around the small, heavy cardboard box as one man sprawled back, winded, into the open doorway, and the other scrambled and half fell down the slippery steps.

His vision wavered, heat and cold tingled through

him in a disorienting torrent, as if he'd just walked into some strange electrical field, and a dizzying sense of déjà vu hit him. He staggered, his vision faded, became overlaid with another—hot blue sky, blinding heat, the dank smell of a river. His gloved hand curled around rain-slick railing, cold metal anchoring him in place as he fought to orient himself, and for a moment he had a sense that he was wearing antique garments, his chest sheathed in a breastplate of thick, toughened leather as hard as wood, the hilt of a sword burning in his hand.

He was vaguely aware of the sprawled man scrambling to his feet, felt a wrench as the cardboard box was ripped from his grasp, then static erupted from his lip mike, and the dizzying conviction that he'd been transported to another place, another time—for however brief a moment—was replaced by a moment of utter clarity.

"Tyler."

His gut twisted, certainty settled in his mind. He should never have left her alone.

He spoke rapidly into the lip mike as he ran down the slick, cobbled path. "Two men, heading north. They've got the jade. I'm going back for Tyler."

Static exploded in his ear. He shoved the mike away from his mouth as he rounded a corner, his gaze skimming the layout of the buildings as he calculated the quickest route between the blocks of units and the thick banks of ornamental plantings. Cursing, he shoved through a thick screen of palm trees.

* * *

The rain finally abated. Tyler wound down the misted window of the car and breathed a sigh of relief as a breeze flowed in, dissipating some of the claustrophobic heat that had built up in the car. She'd wiped the windows several times in an attempt to maintain some kind of a view of the street, and in the end she'd left them alone, because as fast as she wiped they steamed up again and, with rain sliding down the glass, she hadn't been able to see a thing anyway.

She pressed Redial on Cornell's number again. This time, instead of his answering service, she got an engaged signal, which was progress. She checked her watch and resolved to try again in one minute.

In total, only twenty minutes had passed since West and the others had disappeared into the motel complex; it felt like an hour.

Sliding the cell phone into her bag, she hooked the strap over her shoulder, pushed the passenger door open and stepped out onto the street, breathing in the musty tang of wet trees and the flowering shrubs that overhung the sidewalk. Instead of cooling the temperature, the rain had increased the humidity, turning the road into a steam bath. Her skin was clammy with heat. Even her clothes felt damp.

Tyler heard her name called and spun to see a dark figure just metres away. Shock jolted along her spine. She stared in disbelief at a lithe shadow of a man. His gaze fastened on hers, flat and cold, and that first shock of recognition gave way to confusion.

She was used to seeing him in a suit, always neat, always urbane. She'd thought she knew him as well as she knew Richard or Harrison, but this man was a complete stranger.

He lifted his hand, and it was then that she saw the gun.

"Get in the car." The gun centered on a point between her brows. The streetlight glinted coldly off the blunt-nosed end of the barrel. "Driver's seat. Now."

Adrenaline flooded her system, holding her frozen for long seconds, then her mind spun into overdrive. Her fingers tightened on her bag. The eyes locked on hers were icily light and remote—and completely devoid of emotion. She knew nothing about this kind of confrontation except that if she got in the car, that would be it, she wouldn't get out alive. "No."

The gun remained centered on her forehead. Ashley James moved toward her, his step slow, easy.

He was dressed all in black, the clothes snug-fitting, and he held a black briefcase in one hand. In the sleek clothes he looked alien and dangerous; his shoulders broad, his figure leanly muscular and athletic.

She wondered that she hadn't noticed his build before, or the way he moved, but then she'd only ever seen him in a business perspective. Even at social occasions, he had always come across as more neutral than overtly masculine. He'd always been impeccably dressed—seeming older than the mid-thirties she knew him to be—and a little distant, as if he couldn't quite fit in.

His hair was different—dyed platinum-blond and cut in a short spiky style that made him look years younger. He'd also done something to change the color of his eyes. Beneath the yellowish street-lighting, they were a light, icy color instead of the grayish shade she was used to seeing.

"Get the keys out of your bag," he said softly. "Do it slowly, then get in the driver's seat."

Adrenaline continued to flood her system, a constant drip feed that made her heart race and sent fine tremors shaking through her. She knew this game—had seen it played out countless times on the streets—although never with a gun. The gun was hard to dismiss, but the basics of confrontation remained the same. Keep the eye contact steady. Don't move backward, unless you meant to run. "Or what, Ashley?" The soft goad in her voice came naturally, dredged up from a part of herself she'd tried hard to forget. "Are you actually going to shoot me?"

The distant wail of a siren sounded. Ashley's gaze shifted to the street, then back again. The gun didn't waver.

The siren grew louder. The high-pitched ululation made Tyler's heart slam. When she'd been a child that had been a sound to fear—now it could provide the leeway she needed. They were on a reasonably busy road, and it was Saturday night. The vehicle could be an ambulance, but there was every chance it was a police car and that it would come this way, passing within bare metres of them. All she had to do was move closer to the road.

She stepped sideways, not taking her gaze off Ashley. "You attacked me in the garage."

The siren was growing louder by increments, stretching her nerves to breaking point.

Ashley moved sideways, too, but away from the road and the glare of the streetlight, edging into the shadows so that only the pale shape of his face, his shock of blond hair, and the shiny glint of the gun were visible.

"A diversionary tactic. I needed suspicion to be firmly on you before I proceeded to the next step."

Tyler felt sick. "You were going to implicate me in the theft, then kill me so you could get away with the jade?"

His teeth gleamed in the shadows. "Not exactly. The jade was just part of the game. It was valuable to you, so I stole it."

She took a breath. The siren was close, the pulsing sound filling the night. "So this is about me."

"Wrong," he said softly. "It's all about me. I steal from the rich—but I don't just want their jewelry. I like to take everything."

A police car shot past the intersection at the head of the street. The strobing blue-and-red lights flashed down the slick road and the siren began to recede.

Ashley emerged from the shadows. "Get in the car, Tyler, and I'll tell you what I'm going to do to you while you drive."

Chapter 17

Carter took a shortcut through soaking-wet shrubbery, cursing as a branch whipped his cheek, the cut stinging like cold fire. The bad guy had climbed out of one of the windows of the motel unit like a slippery eel, evading capture by a split second. Carter had slid while chasing him, and his ass was wet. Now he was bleeding.

He caught a flash of pale skin, heard a high-pitched curse and a tinny jangle as if a set of car keys had been dropped. Droplets showered down on him as he pushed free of a trailing vine, getting him in the eye.

He caught the man as he wrenched his car door wide. He didn't waste time with words, simply grabbed him by the scruff of the neck, spun him around and clipped him on the jaw. There was no particular finesse involved—but the technique was time-honored. The bad guy went limp and dropped like a stone.

Carter used the man's belt to fasten his hands behind his back, then assessed his options for keeping the guy on hold until the police arrived. In the end, the solution was simple. He did a quick search and confiscated his wallet and spare car keys, located the key that had been dropped on the ground, then dumped the man in the back seat and locked the car.

The vehicle was a late-model sedan—all pretty streamlined curves—the kind that was fitted with a factory security system designed to stop car thieves dead in their tracks. Once the locking device was activated, everything was effectively frozen. The car couldn't be started and the doors and windows couldn't be opened from the inside or out. Nothing would work until the correct key decoded the computerized lock. The design was revolutionary as far as car security was concerned, but it had its drawbacks. The owner of this car was now effectively contained within a prison. He would have to break a window to get out.

A dark shadow condensed out of darkness. Tyler's heart slammed hard against her chest. It was West, and he was walking up behind Ashley as calmly as any pedestrian on the street.

The knowledge must have been mirrored in her

eyes because she saw the moment Ashley realized someone was behind him, and in that moment she knew he would use the gun.

Fear flashed through her, and with it another healthy kick of adrenaline. Her fingers tightened on the bag, every muscle tensed. Ashley's head whipped around. Tyler felt the moment that Ashley's focus left her like a weight lifting, and in that moment she launched the bag.

Adrenaline did strange things. It altered perceptions, so that for an endless moment time seemed to slow, stop; the damp swirl of drizzle, the faint breeze rustling through the leaves and the steady roar of traffic ceased.

The bag connected solidly with Ashley's shoulder, and in that same moment she saw the swift arc of West's hand as it chopped down on Ashley's wrist, instantly followed by the flat sound as a dark fist snapped Ashley's head back. The gun clattered on the pavement, and sound crashed back.

"Are you crazy?" West snapped, fury flashing through him. He grabbed Tyler, pulled her out of the light, into the cover of the shrubs, and wrapped his arms around her. He didn't question his instinct to go for cover; he'd counted four bad guys, and they'd all scrambled in different directions.

He cupped Tyler's face and turned it toward him. The gun pointed at her was his worst nightmare. "Are you crazy, throwing that bag at him?" he demanded, not caring that he was repeating himself. "You could have been shot."

Her face was a pale oval in the deep pooling shadows. She was tense and too still, her skin unnaturally cold as if all the blood had drained from her face.

"He was going to kill me anyway."

The stark flatness of her words sent a chill down his spine. He hadn't gotten a good look at the guy he'd decked, and he hadn't recognized him, but he recognized what was happening to Tyler; she was going into shock again. He grasped her shoulders and shook her slightly, trying to get her to snap out of it. "He had a gun trained on you. That didn't mean he was going to fire it."

In most confrontations with firearms, the gun never got fired. And if people who were involved in those confrontations knew the statistics of their chances of actually being hit by a bullet if a firearm was discharged, they wouldn't be so petrified.

"No." Her voice still had that stark, eerie flatness. A small shudder jerked through her. Her gaze finally connected with his, but his relief was short-lived. "He meant to kill me. This was personal."

West swore softly beneath his breath. "Stay here. Don't move out of the shadows, and keep your movements to a minimum."

His gaze swept the sidewalk, looking for the gun. When he saw the Bernadelli, his belly went cold; the direct link with the theft of the jade and their stalker, chilling.

He nudged the Bernadelli farther away from the perp with his booted foot, and studied the still form of the man lying on the sidewalk. He was average height, his body lean and toned. The black clothes and boots were practical B and E gear. The anarchistic spiky blond cut was the only aberration.

Ashley James. The extent of the deception made West go still inside. He'd met James briefly on a few occasions, and each time the overwhelming impression had been the utter absence of personality.

Ashley's lids flickered, his eerily light eyes settled on West, and the part of himself that he'd kept hidden poured from him, an overwhelming presence of cold, a basic amorality that would always keep him separate from most of the human race. All the hairs at West's nape lifted and in that moment he knew James intimately.

Before James could recover fully, West flipped him on his stomach and held him in a wrestling hold, his arm tightened on James's neck, pressing on his carotid—not enough to kill him, but enough to put him out and keep him out for a while.

James grunted, fighting the hold.

"Don't bother," West said coldly. "You screwed up. You picked the wrong victim. You'll be locked up so long you'll be an old man before you get out, if at all, because Interpol are going to send your DNA profile to every major law enforcement agency on the planet. If you so much as dropped a hair, left a fingerprint or a smear of body fluids anywhere that evidence was collected, they're going to find out.''

West felt James go limp. He kept the pressure on the carotid, counting the seconds, because the brain could only survive so long without oxygen, and he didn't want to kill James. When he was satisfied that he would stay unconscious, he released the hold and sat back on his haunches, feeling sick to his stomach.

The sound of footsteps pounding on the pavement jerked his head up. He heard the harsh rasp of the man's breathing, saw the flap of a jacket, the shape of a gun, and flowed to his feet.

He saw Tyler turn, startled, the bright swing of her hair beneath the streetlight. Adrenaline flooded his system. His heart slammed against his chest and he dove. Everything seemed to flow in slow motion as he wrapped his arms around her and took her down to the pavement.

The report of a handgun from close range snapped in his ears. He clamped Tyler tight against him and rolled until they were behind the car, his chest tight with panic. A car swished past, the beam of the headlights catching them in its glare. The road was wet, the gutters still running with water. Tyler was lying half beneath him, legs tangled with his, hair spilled over her face. She made an odd gasping sound, and pushed at his chest.

West's weight finally shifted off Tyler and her chest convulsed as she tried to breathe, but it was as if her entire system had closed down, her throat clamped, lungs burning.

West snapped a question at her, then another, his hands moving rapidly over her body as he searched for a wound.

His gaze locked with hers, dark and burning. "Damn it," he roared, *"talk to me."*

Her head spun, and she began to drift. Distantly, she heard West cursing, then his mouth locked over hers. The pressure of his breath made her chest convulse again, the loss of control so complete that she felt as boneless as a rag doll. Her vision dimmed, then abruptly oxygen flooded her lungs. A paroxysm of coughing shook her, and Tyler found herself turned on her side. West's hands gripped her face, his dark eyes glared into hers. "Talk to me."

She gulped in a breath and swallowed the urge to cough. "I'm not hurt—at least I don't think I am. Just winded."

Relief flooded West. He hadn't found a wound, her pulse was good, but a shot had been fired and he'd panicked. Tyler hadn't been hit. Relief loosened off his tension, then a burning pain registered. He'd been told that getting shot felt a lot like being punched—sometimes like being kicked by a mule. The shock wave hit, numbing the area, and a lot of guys had a period of confusion about whether or not they'd taken a bullet at all before the pain kicked in.

He gritted his teeth as he slowly straightened, the pain increasing with every second.

His uncanny run of luck had finished. Tyler hadn't been hit, but he had.

Tyler scrambled to her feet. West's hand shot out to help her; she brushed it aside. She hadn't missed his wince when he'd gotten up.

"You're hurt."

He stripped off his T-shirt and began folding it into a pad. "It's nothing. Much."

There was blood on his hand, and she noticed his face was pale and his eyes were glazed. Over the past couple of days she'd come to recognize that look; she'd seen it often enough in her own eyes in the mirror. Now he was in mild shock.

"Let me see," she demanded fiercely.

He turned and she saw the frayed tear in his pants, the seep of blood, but it was hard to gauge just how much blood because West's pants were black, and the light wasn't good. The tear itself ran almost parallel to the waistband.

"It's a graze...I think. You're going to have to take your pants off so I can see properly."

"It can wait." He pressed the T-shirt to the wound with one hand, and pulled her close with the other, burying his face at the nape of her neck.

His skin was hot and damp, the beat of his heart steady against her, and he smelled delicious—sweaty and male and alive. She noticed he was trembling almost as much as she was.

He lifted his head and found her mouth with his,

the kiss hard. Tyler wound her arms around his waist and hung on.

A tiny burst of static sounded. West lifted his head, he pulled his lip mike to his mouth, and talked into it. "That was Carter. He's locked one of them in a car."

Minutes later, Gray, Blade and Carter emerged out of darkness. Gray was holding a squirming figure by the scruff of the neck and herding him along. Tyler recognized the gunman who'd just shot West.

Gray pointed at the sidewalk. "Sit," he barked. "He was babbling about a gun. We searched him, but didn't find it."

He glanced at West as the man meekly complied, and then swore. "He *shot* you."

West kept his eye on James who was still unconscious. "Just barely."

"West's been hit?" Carter closed the distance between them in two strides, pushed West's hand away, lifted the pad and examined the graze. "It's shallow, and you've lost some blood, but not much." He shook his head. "I don't believe it. Whole terrorist squads have tried to hit you and missed."

West reapplied the pad, wincing because even in the short time that had passed the wound had stiffened up. "I don't think he was trying to hit anything."

The man was an amateur—that had been clear just by the way he'd held the weapon. If he'd hit anything, it had been by mistake. In a further escalation of his panic, he'd either dropped the gun, or thrown it away.

Carter's expression was grim. "Who is he?" Accidental discharge or not, the man was dangerous. He could have killed West.

Gray extracted a wallet from the man on the ground. He examined a driver's licence. "Ernest Wallace." He made a sound of disbelief. "There's a business card here, says Ernie sells insurance when he's not shooting the butts off ex-SAS sniper commanders."

Blade stared at the man sitting cross-legged on the wet sidewalk, his face pale. Ernie wasn't wearing dark, nondescript clothing that would help make him invisible in the dark; he was apparently still dressed for work, wearing a cream striped polyester shirt, a red-and-cream striped tie and a brown suit. The suit looked as if it was also made of polyester. Blade hadn't thought anyone wore brown polyester these days.

Fashion mistakes aside, the sheer scale of the amateurism was upsetting. They had been taken down by a group of suits driving four-door sedans who, if the information they'd garnered from Ernie was representative, only practiced larceny in their spare time.

Blade nudged Ashley with one booted foot. "What about this guy? You didn't give him brain damage, did you?"

West eyed Ashley coldly and briefly outlined just

who and what Ashley was. ''The damage was done before I ever touched him.''

Blade glanced at the gleam of the Bernadelli, which was just discernible at the edge of the pooling shadows beneath the shrubbery, his gaze dark and cold. He knew all he wanted to know about Ashley James. He was a thief, probably a rapist and a murderer, and he'd stolen West's gun to implicate him in the crimes he'd planned. West had stopped him, but if James's eyelids so much as flickered, Blade would happily break his jaw. Grimly, he pulled a pair of cuffs from his back pocket and snapped them around Ashley's wrists.

West shook his head. ''Where did you get those?''

Blade grinned. ''My cousin's son mail-ordered them from some outfit in the States. And before you ask, no, you can't borrow them.''

A cell phone buzzed. Tyler fished her phone out of her bag. ''It's Richard. They've finally got hold of Cornell. He's on his way.''

West took the phone and spoke in quick terse sentences. When he terminated the conversation and handed the phone back to Tyler, his expression was blank and cold. ''They'll be here in five with a full team.''

Blade leaned on West's car, wincing as he did so. He was fit, he still ran most mornings, and he rode a lot, but his back was aching. He must have pulled a muscle diving at the scrawny guy in the checked suit—the one that had got away. A checked suit.

Somehow that was more of a crime than polyester. It was hard to admit, but... "I'm getting too old for this."

Gray caught his eye. "You're younger than I am."

Carter grinned. "Mate, almost everyone's younger than you."

"Oh, yeah, that's it. Rub it in."

Minutes later a police car pulled into the space in front of West's car, the signature red-and-blue lights strobing the area. West glanced at Ashley, who was now conscious, but securely cuffed to a steel mailbox post. "Here comes the paperwork."

Ray Cornell climbed out of the cruiser, followed by Farrell, who'd been driving. That figured. Ray was a hard ass from way back, but Farrell had an edge that could cut steel. If she wanted to drive, West would sure as hell let her drive.

Cornell eyed West with disbelief. "*You're* the person who got shot?" He glanced at Farrell. "Did someone put hallucinogen into the coffee?"

Farrell lifted a brow. "Like we'd ever get that lucky. Maybe then, we could pretend it tasted good. But if you're sensitive to artificial sweeteners, honey, right now you're flying."

West winced as Carter slapped a first aid kit he'd pulled from his car on the bonnet of the Saab and eased his pants down far enough to check the damage.

Farrell surveyed West's bronzed buttock with interest. Hey, she had a guy, but there was no harm in looking—and the butt *was* legendary. Her shoulders shook slightly. "Need an ambulance?"

Carter probed and pressed.

The breath hissed in between West's teeth. "If Carter tries to jab me with a needle, place the call."

Blade eyed the seeping wound as Carter applied nonstick pads and taped the area. "I don't think you're in any danger of getting morphine. Carter's miserly with it—likes to save that stuff for special occasions."

Cornell lifted a hand to his mouth, then gave up trying to suppress the grin. "If this isn't a special occasion I don't know what is." He eyed both of the captives. "So, who got your cherry?"

West steeled himself against the humor. After years of having a reputation as a hard, cold bastard, of having an uncanny luck in the field, he'd been shot by a rank amateur. He could see the funny side. All the same, he was glad he was out of the military because he would never have lived this one down.

"He's an insurance rep called Ernest Wallace."

"Not on Interpol's Most Wanted List, huh?"

Blade leaned against the car. "Looks like he's been in business for all of five minutes."

Cornell briefly examined Wallace, who was in the process of being escorted into the back of a cruiser. "You never can discount the amateur factor. A little bit of knowledge is a dangerous thing."

West eased his pants up and fastened them, relieved Carter had finished so quickly. He was a damn good medic, but a little on the scary side with his bedside manner. Out in the field he took no prisoners. When it came to combat medicine, the same attitude applied. ''Any more clichés, Cornell?''

''Just one,'' he said evenly. ''Try not to get caught with your pants down again. Especially not when Farrell's around. That woman's got a long memory.''

Chapter 18

Ashley was cuffed and sitting in the back of the cruiser with two uniformed policemen. Farrell was overseeing the legal processing of the other two men as they were cuffed, read their rights and bundled into a second police car.

The radio blared static as Cornell finished a brief conversation and replaced the mouthpiece on its cradle. He pulled on latex gloves and bagged the gun. "Nice weapon."

West's voice was cold. "It's mine. James broke into my house and stole it."

Cornell went still. He'd dealt with some certifiably weird cases—enough of them to doubt he could ever be surprised by the myriad distortions of the criminal mind again, but West had just surprised him. They were ninety-nine-point-nine percent sure they had their jade thief—and a lot more. "When did your gun go missing?"

"I don't know exactly. I didn't check the safe until tonight—"

"—and you have a computerized locking system."

"You got it."

Cornell slipped the gun in beside James's briefcase, which was sitting encased in a plastic evidence bag in the boot of the cruiser. "Well, at least *that's* consistent. Take a look at this."

He unzipped the plastic around the briefcase and flipped the lid on the case.

Tyler felt sick. "That's my laptop."

Even though she knew Ashley was the perpetrator of everything that had gone wrong from the theft of the jade onwards, actually seeing the proof was shocking.

Cornell unzipped a flap, lifted out an envelope, looked at the contents, then tipped several snapshots out onto the surface of the laptop. There was a brief silence.

West shook his head. "That's twisted."

Tyler looked at the photographs of herself. She recognized them, although she hadn't looked at them in years. They had been stored in a photograph album in her lounge, which meant Ashley had broken into her apartment when she *hadn't* been home. And maybe more than once.

She shook her head. "I don't get it. He's worked for Laine's for years. In that time he's never shown any interest in me, and even less in jade. Ashley works with diamonds."

Cornell's gaze was hooded. "Ask me in a couple of days, or maybe make that ten years. There's never been anything straightforward about this investigation, and something tells me that sonovabitch isn't going to make it any easier."

West smiled coldly. Farrell was reading Ashley James his rights and taking her time over it. If that didn't scare him, he didn't know what would.

Farrell asked Ashley where the jade was and got a finger for her trouble.

"Lose the sign language, buddy." She slammed the door of the police cruiser, looking ticked off, slapped her notebook closed and slipped it into her pocket. "Man, I hate loose ends. I *want* that jade."

She shot James a goading look. "Like the after-hours mafia aren't going to tell all, anyway."

Ashley didn't respond or acknowledge Farrell in any way, his expression as cold and blank as marble.

Farrell flashed West and Tyler a grin, the light of battle in her eyes. "Life is good. Oh boy, am I going to enjoy this."

The statements took time. The crime might take just minutes to commit, but the wheels of justice were driven by detail.

Two hours after entering Auckland Central, Cornell walked into the interview room where West, Tyler, Blade, Gray, Carter and Richard were drinking coffee.

"He hasn't confessed, but we don't need a confession. We've got more than enough to hold him with the testimony and evidence we've collected. The wash-up on the jade is going to take a little longer, since we didn't actually catch him with it in his possession, but we've got the lab boys working on his briefcase. With any luck, they'll find material that will directly link James to the jade. If not, we've got him on motivation and opportunity. And in any case, Reed and Wallace are cooperating fully. Reed's already identified James's voice."

Tyler cradled her cup between her hands, even though the coffee had long gone cold. "And the jade?"

"Reed gave us the name and the flight number. The jet's still on the tarmac and won't be leaving until the jade's recovered."

Tyler felt herself go limp with relief. "So it's finished."

Cornell lifted a brow. "All except for the publicity." Their boy was a rarity. The press had already got a whiff of the story and were pressing for details. In a couple of hours the place would be overrun with reporters and TV crews.

Cornell shoved a hand through his hair, not sure how to handle the next part of the conversation. The series of crimes that had happened around Tyler

Laine had been diverse and mystifying, and had happened so fast they'd struggled to keep up. Every time he'd done a computer search he'd kept hitting the same list of unsolved crimes, spread across different countries, but all with enough similarities in common that they had been grouped. After the break-in at Tyler's flat, the pattern had become too strong to ignore.

"James led a double life. During the day he was a respected businessman, but in private, he dealt in larceny. We've searched his house. It's empty, although his car was still garaged, with luggage in the boot. He was packed, ready to leave the country, and stashed in a concealed compartment in his suitcase we found an alternative identity—a passport, credit cards, air ticket and travel insurance documents for one Edward Hammel. If you hadn't caught him when you did, he would have disappeared into thin air.

"Interpol are now investigating Edward Hammel who just happens to be a fine gems assessor in Geneva. He owns a residence and has a numbered Swiss account and a safety deposit box that so far we haven't been able to touch—but Interpol are working it through the courts. It might take a couple of years, but eventually they'll get access. From what we can make out, Ashley James has been responsible for most of the major diamond thefts in the southern hemisphere for the past ten years. We ran all the diamond thefts we have through the computer, and came up with a percentage that fit his M.O. Now all we have to do is compare the date and location of the thefts to James's overseas jaunts, and see if we come up with any matches. He went overseas on a regular basis to buy diamonds for Laine's, but I'm willing to bet he did a little moonlighting on some of those trips. He isn't admitting to any of it—and we don't expect to nail him on all counts—but we'll have enough to put him away.

"Even if he'd never stolen a thing, attempted murder is a serious crime—it'll be years before he surfaces on the street. And when we're finished with him there's an additional list of warrants for his arrest.

"If we're right about our boy, he's wanted in South Africa, Australia, Papua New Guinea, Chile, Ecuador and Colombia. Hell, even the Samoans want him."

West set his cup down. "What's he wanted for primarily?"

Cornell met West's icy gaze, and saw the knowledge there before he answered. "Murder."

West went cold inside. "He's a serial killer."

Sometime while they'd been in the station it had rained, and now steam lifted off the pavement making the gray pre-dawn seem even more secretive and mysterious. The first touch of light in the east, reminded West of another dawn just over a month ago, but this wasn't Port Moresby, Papua New Guinea, thank God. The morning might be gray and the street might be slick with rain, but Ponsonby Road, with its cafés and interior decorating shops possessed a shabby, upmarket elegance that was a far cry from the feeding grounds of arms dealers.

West leaned on Tyler's car and pulled her close. He felt the first touch of the sun as it burned away the mist and the grayness, touching everything with a delicate, transparent, light, and he thought about Port Moresby again.

For a moment he felt the isolation he'd felt in Port Moresby, but this time there was no blood, no death and the woman he was holding was alive, and his.

He ran his fingers through Tyler's hair, careful of the tender area around her scar. The bright strands felt cool and silky, almost as good as her skin.

She wrapped her arms around his neck, her mouth melted into his, and the tension inside him unwound. Oh yeah, this was what he wanted. *This.*

Dimly he noticed that the traffic was beginning to flow. Unlike the industrial area at Port Moresby, Ponsonby Road was busy—an urban hub of activity not far from the central business district of town. He lifted his mouth, touched his forehead against hers. "I'm never letting you out of my sight again. I go away for five minutes—"

"Five years—"

"—and you somehow manage to attract the attention of a serial killer."

"I didn't want you to leave."

"I didn't want to go."

She pulled back slightly. Her green eyes fastened on his. ''Does that mean you're in love with me?''

His heart slammed hard in his chest; *love.* He had difficulty even thinking about that word, let alone saying it. For most of his life he'd been defending himself from it. He hadn't wanted friendships, and he hadn't wanted a wife or family because he didn't ever think anyone could—knowing his past, knowing the way he was inside—love him.

He swallowed, but even so, when he spoke his voice sounded husky and hollow. ''I've been crazy, head over heels in love with you ever since I first met you. Why do you think Carter clucks around me like an old hen with her only chick?''

Tyler blinked, for a moment unable to take in the simple phrases, then what he'd said sank in.

He had been in love with her all along.

She went hot and cold, all the fine hairs at her nape stood on end, and abruptly, as if some internal focus had readjusted, she saw him.

The unsettling directness of his amber gaze was still the same, the shape of his mouth, that tough male jaw, but something had changed, the alteration as invisible as an electric current: powerful, but *there.* With a jolt, she realized that he was letting her see him. He had dropped his tough inner defences; the cool, impenetrable barrier to his emotions was gone.

Her chest clenched on a hard pulse of emotion, the ache raising goose bumps and searing nerve endings.

Too late to wish fiercely that she'd ignored that barrier before, but she now had what she'd always needed. For the first time she was certain of him. Like the subtle flow that had emanated from the jade, she could *feel* him, the moment he'd literally opened up to her powerful and immediate, as if in that moment a link had been forged.

She had her barriers but West had a fortress. "You're like me, only worse."

"You had what I was missing. Courage."

Tears burned the back of her eyes. "Not enough to reach you."

He framed her face with his hands. "You did nothing but reach me. I left, but I couldn't stop thinking about you. It got so that I couldn't concentrate, couldn't work."

West didn't tell her that if he'd stayed in the SAS any longer he was certain he would have ended up dead because he'd gotten so used to walking toward death, he'd stopped caring about living.

Fierceness gripped him. He didn't want that anymore; he'd found something better. "You know what I'm like."

"Difficult."

"But you'll take me back?"

"I'll take you any way I can get you." Her gaze told him that not only would she take him back; this time she would hold him.

His arms tightened convulsively around Tyler. He buried his face in her hair. His chest was so tight, he could barely breathe; his eyes were burning. The last time he'd cried had been when he and his mother had been evicted from her flat, and she'd told him she couldn't look after him anymore. She had walked in one direction, he'd walked in the other. He had been five.

The morning gradually lightened, the glow from the sun warming his back, unlocking some of his tension. A faint morning breeze sprang up, soft with condensation and laced with the scents of the city and he finally lifted his head and loosened his hold.

Tyler shifted in his grip, as if, like him, she didn't want to let go. Her mouth touched on his, clung.

A horn sounded. Someone yelled out from a passing car.

A jogger pounded past and whistled.

A skinny dog planted its rump beside West. He was black and tan, and looked as though he would have been happier in a paddock full of sheep instead of sitting on the dusty sidewalk of a city. The dog lifted his head and eyed West with soft, dark eyes.

"That's it, we're out of here." West unlocked the car and opened the passenger door for Tyler. "I'm sick of sharing you. We're going somewhere isolated. No people, no guns, no family, no friends. Absolutely no friends."

"There's only one thing wrong with that scenario." She took the keys from his fingers. "You're injured, and I'm driving."

West felt the smile build up inside him, roll

through him like warmth and honey and sunlight, as he eased into the passenger seat. For the first time in years—no, cancel that, in his life—he felt happy.

West noticed the dog continued to watch them with big, soulful eyes as Tyler pulled out from the curb.

He fastened his seat belt, wincing at the pain the movement caused. Carter had padded the graze up, and West had swallowed a couple of painkillers at the station, but the area still throbbed. He leaned his head back on the headrest and glanced in the side rear vision mirror. "There's just one problem."

Tyler was already pulling a U-turn. She threw him a glance, as they headed back toward the dog. "You have to bathe it."

West climbed out and walked around to the dog. "It's a him. The dog is a him."

"Okay, you have to bathe *him.*"

West opened the back door. The dog jumped in and made himself at home, settling down, tongue lolling happily, as if he owned the car.

They had a marriage and two cats, and now they had a dog. All they needed were kids to complete the package. That thought should scare the hell out of him, but instead he felt a dizzying sense of anticipation. Fatherhood. It was a scary assignment, but he'd always been a risk taker, and this particular mission was right down his alley.

Epilogue

Tyler propped pillows behind her, careful not to disturb West, who was still sleeping, slipped on her spectacles and reached for the book that was on her bedside table. It was too early to get up, and she knew she wouldn't go back to sleep. Lately she'd been restless…unsettled. She'd had trouble sleeping, she'd even had trouble concentrating at work.

Smothering a yawn, she flipped pages slowly, studying the exquisite line drawings of neolithic jade and bronze artifacts. She turned a page and her stomach tightened on a jolt of recognition.

The line drawing was simple, a jade ko, or dagger, with the distinctive solar symbol engraved on the hilt.

The book was a volume that had been compiled

by a British archaeologist who'd spent time in China during the eighteenth century, long before China had closed its doors to the western world. In itself it was a rare and esoteric publication, but it didn't constitute proof that any of these artifacts actually existed, or that provenance had ever been established. Even so, it was another link to be explored, another layer to the mystery of the jade.

She read the brief description that accompanied the drawing, and her heart thumped in her chest as she found a brief reference to the early solar warrior fraternities. For a moment she relived again the humming energy that had radiated from the jade, and a sense of certainty settled inside her.

She set the book down on her lap and contemplated West's bronzed back, his relaxed sprawl in the bed. It was early, and he needed to sleep, and he would probably think she'd gone crazy even to think what she was thinking, but she needed to talk about this now.

She gave his bare shoulder a shake. He grunted and burrowed deeper into the pillow.

She shook a little harder. This time there was even less response. Tyler eyed the deep groove of his spine, the slow rhythm of his breathing, and tenderness caught at her. No flight or fight response there.

That was another of the changes she'd noticed in West. He *slept,* when years ago, after they'd first been married, she'd almost never seen him deeply asleep. Generally she'd found that if she'd been awake, he was, too, as if even the slight alteration in her breathing had alerted him.

She shook him again, and this time he did respond, rolling onto his back.

Too bad if there was danger.

His eyes didn't flicker, and the slow rise and fall of his chest didn't alter, but as suddenly as if someone had flicked a switch, she knew he was awake.

She took a deep breath and let it out slowly. "I think the jade could have belonged to you."

He took so long answering that for a moment she wondered if he'd drifted back to sleep again, then, "The jade's thousands of years old. I was born in—"

"Reincarnation," she cut in, wondering if she *was* going a little crazy. She was an academic, and while the flow of history and the possibility of reincarnation had always fascinated her, she had no scientific basis for belief—just a funny, fizzy feeling in the pit of her stomach. "I'm talking reincarnation."

West forced one eye open. It was Sunday morning, and overbright at that. He checked the bedside clock and groaned. Six-thirty. "I was trying to sleep."

"Hah."

She held a book open in front of his face. All he could make out was a dark blur. Six-thirty. It would be at least another half hour before his eyes wanted to see anything. He focused on a distinctive symbol, which was similar to the one on the jade artifacts.

He switched his attention to Tyler. Her green gaze was shadowed in the early-morning light, and unexpectedly fierce. With her tanned skin and tawny hair, she reminded him of a tigress, and delight surged through him at the sheer pleasure of waking up next to his wife. "Anyone ever tell you you're cute when you're mad?"

"No one alive."

West sat up. It was an effort.

Tyler made a small sound. "Don't do that."

Now what was wrong? Lately Tyler had become distracted and picky. In all the years he'd known her she had never been picky.

"Don't flash your chest at me, okay? You know it wrecks my concentration."

Okay. *Now* he was waking up.

"Call it women's intuition," she said flatly. "That jade belonged to you."

"Whoever it belonged to," he said flatly, "I'm glad it's gone."

The jade had survived several months in limbo while it had been picked over by forensics, and argued over by the academics. A lot of theories had been tossed around about how it had arrived in New Zealand, and when and how it had come to end up in a burial cave. Maori taonga, or precious objects, were traditionally passed on, and not put in the ground unless there was some spiritual reason to do so.

Academic arguments aside, the three objects had finally been gifted to the people of New Zealand, and were presently on tour, doing the rounds of several major overseas museums.

West had been more than pleased to see the jade gone. It had been the catalyst for too much trouble for him to want it anywhere near Tyler. Other than that disorienting sense of another time—that he'd experienced when the jade had been shoved at his chest outside the motel room, he felt no sense of connection with it. And every time he thought about what Ashley James had planned, using the jade as the first stratagem in his game, he went cold inside.

Ashley James was locked up, and it would be a long time before he hit the streets again, if ever. According to Cornell, they were still compiling evidence, and likely to continue to do so for years to come.

Apparently James had used his entrée into the exclusive world of diamond buying to ferret out information on who was buying high-grade gems, then he would plan a side trip and execute the theft. He had a policy of never stealing from his suppliers or Laine's, which made sense. Why destroy the source for the sake of one crime that would finish him in the diamond trade?

His thefts were strictly from people who had no inside contacts with the diamond trade, and he had a penchant for stealing from the very wealthy. The problem with tracking all of Ashley's crimes was that, while his modus operandi—characterized by a methodical stalking of a victim, followed by hi-tech sabotage of lighting and security systems to facilitate the crime—remained the same, the nature of the crimes had changed dramatically.

It seemed that, while the financial returns were great, the thrill of stealing diamonds didn't hold James for long. The design of his crimes became more elaborate, and the theft became secondary as he factored in the rape of the woman he was robbing. The stalking and the rapes became progressively more violent, until he finally crossed the line and added murder to his repertoire.

When he stole the jade and stalked Tyler, the aberration in his M.O. had confused the police and Interpol for a time because there was no diamond involved, but, essentially, the symbolism of what Ashley James was doing hadn't changed. He would invade the homes of the rich and steal an object they valued highly, then he would teach them how worthless the object, and all of their wealth and power were, as he proceeded to take everything from them.

Cornell had gone so far as to suggest that in this case Ashley had shifted out of his pattern even further by fixating on Tyler and *waiting* for her to acquire a diamond. When she hadn't shown any interest in his gem of choice, he'd had to take what would hurt her the most: the jade.

The other aberration in James's crime, was that for the first time he was breaking his own self-imposed rule of not stealing from his employer.

The only possible motivation for him to expose

himself in that way was that he had decided to retire from the diamond business. This was verified by the fact that he'd packed all of his household effects, and was leaving the country under an assumed identity. Ashley James was on the point of ceasing to exist when they'd caught him. He had been booked out on a flight that evening, and had taken time out to deliver the jade, a victim of his own rule that he must complete his crime, and in doing so further affirm his dominance over his victim by collecting payment.

If he'd simply dropped the jade in the sea and walked away, he would probably be free right now, and Tyler would still be at risk.

West propped himself on one elbow and surveyed Tyler. "How's this for intuition? You're pregnant."

"I'm not. I can't be."

"You are. It's not as if we haven't been trying. When was your last period?"

She blinked, her eyes owlish behind her spectacles and he grinned. Those prim and proper little professor's glasses propped on her delicate nose drove him wild every time.

"I can't be."

"If you aren't pregnant, *I'm* checking into the clinic."

She ran her hand down over her flat belly and he realized how vulnerable she was about the subject. Her childhood had been as traumatic as his own. The gift of a baby—the staggering responsibility of having charge of a child's life—held an extra dimension of fear for both of them because they knew just how much could go wrong.

"You can't be sure."

Tyler pressed on her abdomen again. She *had* noticed small changes in her body, but she'd kept her suspicions to herself—half afraid that she was imagining the changes because she wanted this baby so much. She'd even managed to restrain herself from buying a test kit because she couldn't bear the disappointment if it was too soon for a positive result to show.

West propped his head on one hand, not about to be diverted from his discovery. "Your body's changed. Your breasts are larger."

She lifted off her glasses and put them on the bedside table. Without the spectacles she looked younger and infinitely more vulnerable. "You've been reading up on the subject."

"Bet on it." He was suddenly absolutely certain. "You're pregnant."

She was silent for a moment, and he could feel the knowledge—the certainty—growing, expanding, settling between them, as fragile and soft as the morning light.

He pulled her close beside him. Her head settled on his shoulder. He felt peaceful, yet curiously alert as they lay, immersed in a silence that was comfortable, though oddly electrified—as if the change that had taken place somehow existed subtly in the air, binding them even closer, and for a moment the déjà vu shimmered in his mind, sliding and elusive, so that for the briefest moment he was certain he'd held her this way before, felt this way before, even though he knew he never had.

The memory of that moment with the jade resurfaced. He considered, then discarded it. The past was the past. Maybe the jade had linked them in some mysterious way in another time, another life, and maybe what had happened had been sheer coincidence. What was important was now.

Fierce emotion filled him. Second chance, third chance or twentieth, what mattered was that they were together, and this time he wasn't walking away, and he wasn't letting go.

She shifted, propping her chin on her hand, her eyes gimlet-green in the sunlight, and he had the sudden suspicion that he was about to be wound up.

She poked a finger at his chest. "It's your fault."

It took a moment for West to register that Tyler was referring to the pregnancy. "Of course it's my fault," he muttered, abruptly incensed by the illogical comment. "If it was anyone else's, I'd have to go kill somebody."

A delighted grin split her face and he realized he'd been done.

"You know what, West, you're easy. So *easy.*"

Amusement twitched the corner of his mouth.

She had more to say on the subject of women's intuition and the fact that *she* was supposed to know first, not him, and then the morning blurred and passed and West reflected that this was the way it was going to be.

The Lombard kids, who they'd been baby-sitting on occasion, must have been training his wife in standard terrorist tactics when he wasn't looking, which didn't leave much time. When they weren't making love, they were going to be arguing and bickering and playing like a couple of kids—hopefully for the next fifty or so years. On top of that they were going to have a bunch of kids. The noise and chaos would be horrendous.

God help him. It was going to be fun.

* * * * *